J F SNE
Downright Dencey
Snedeker, Caroline Dale,
1871-1956.

WITHDRAWN

MAR 20 2014

D1206265

ALSO BY CAROLINE DALE SNEDEKER

The Spartan
The Perilous Seat
Theras and His Town
The Beckoning Road (sequel to *Downright Dencey*)
The Forgotten Daughter
Uncharted Ways
The White Isle
Luke's Quest
A Triumph for Flavius
Lysis Goes to the Play

Downright
Dencey

Caroline Dale Snedeker

Illustrations by Maginel Wright Barney

Bethlehem Books • Ignatius Press
Bathgate, N.D.   San Francisco

First Bethlehem Books printing June, 2003
Second Bethlehem Books printing January, 2009

© 1927 Caroline Dale Snedeker

Cover art © 2003 by Roseanne Sharpe
Cover design by Davin Carlson

All rights reserved

ISBN 978-1-883937-79-9
Library of Congress Catalog Number: 2003105078

Bethlehem Books • Ignatius Press
10194 Garfield Street South
Bathgate, North Dakota 58216
www.bethlehembooks.com
1-800 757 6831

Printed in the United States on acid free paper

To

My Sister and Beloved Encourager

Nina Parke Stillwell

this book is inscribed

Preface

IN NAMING the characters of this story I have chosen real Nantucket surnames with fictitious Christian names. All the characters are fictitious, though I have given to one of them a historical Nantucket experience. The chapter "Someone Is Hungry" is a true Quaker incident, though it did not happen in Nantucket. I have used the former name State Street instead of the present Main Street. The Coffin School was founded about seven years later than I have indicated in my story. Its first building was on Fair and Lyon streets. It was always a remarkable school, having fine teachers.

My deep gratitude is due to Miss Mary Starbuck for many interesting and constructive suggestions and for guarding me from errors into which the Off-Islander must inevitably fall.

Caroline Dale Snedeker

Contents

BOOK ONE

BOOK TWO

BOOK THREE

BOOK ONE

1. *Dionis Throws the Stone*

THE QUAKER CHILDREN, going along toward school, paused and sniffed delighted noses. The warm air of the little Nantucket street was shot through with vigor and challenge; the breeze smelt of the purity of a thousand miles of open water. Spring was come. The boys were progressing by means of a game of leapfrog in keeping with the season. But the girls walked with a decorousness due partly to admonition, partly to the flowing skirts, and the stays with inch-wide whale-bones, which held their childish bodies slenderly erect. All of a piece were they with the fan-topped doorways and the white picket fences which so carefully enclosed the tiny front plots.

Below them, in full view of the street's cosiness, spread the spring-lighted sea, violet-misted and endless. The children gazed toward it, but only to sight a brig, delicately small in the distance, standing round the Point.

For ships were news.

Now the children turned from North Water Street uptown along Federal, passing the open lot where, a generation later, was to be built the pretty Athenæum. Here along the grassy space stood rows of whale-oil casks. The boys whacked them as they passed, ringing out interesting sounds, high, low, medium, each barrel a different sepulchral tone. Charming instrument for their spring mood!

"Be careful, Dionis," cautioned one little girl to her companion. "Thee flipped thy dress right against a cask. Why, there's a spot."

"Oh, dear!" Dionis looked in consternation. "Those horrid smelly things, and Mother'll punish me again."

"I'll clean it for thee. Thee come home with me after school," urged the other helpfully.

Dionis forgot to thank her, for at that moment something caught her eye, and her mind leaped off on a new interest. It was nothing more than an ivy vine growing out of a rift in a stone wall.

"Look, Hopestill," she cried, eagerly stooping to touch the hardy little thing. "Father told me something wonderful about this ivy."

"That little spindling sprig? Why, that's nothing wonderful."

"Yes, 'tis. It's grown quite a bit since Father was here. I've looked at it every time I go by. Father says it will split the stone wall wide apart, because you see it is alive."

"Alive! My pussy cat is alive, but not that thing, not really."

"Well, I guess thy pussy cat couldn't claw open the stones and the ivy can."

"That's silly, Dencey Coffyn. I don't care if thy father did say it, I'm going to ask my father," declared Hopestill. "This very afternoon."

Dionis made no answering appeal to authority. Her father was three thousand miles away on the West Coast, looking for whales. Dionis must stand upon her own feet.

"No," she maintained. "I know it. The roots . . ."

They turned now into State Street.* Here the mild morning trading was in progress at the little stores. Sailors in their pea-jackets and floppy trousers rolled up the street and stared boredly. And here a tributary stream of school goers met the little Quaker band.

These other children came swarming up from the crowded region of docks and tidal streets—the boys of the Fragment Society School. Democratic Quakerism had yet its strata and its orders, and this was the lowest. To go to the charity school of the Fragment Society was indeed a taint. These ragamuffins knew it and were therefore brazen.

And were not these North Water Street children their special enemies, for did not these go to the newly founded Coffin School where none but ancestral Coffin blood might attend? Were they not all high-nosed aristocrats? It was a new feud but thoroughly vigorous. A low chanting of ribald song was heard:

> If I was a Coffin, I'd go in the ground,
> For that is the place where coffins are found.
>> Bury 'em deep
>> Or out they'll peep
> Bury the Coffins deep in the ground.
>> Bury 'em. Bury 'em. Bury 'em.

Sons of the non-fighting Quakers turned defensively.

"Ho! Fragmenters! Fragmenters! Come on, we'll trounce ye," they yelled back, down the sloping street.

[*Now the famous Main Street of Nantucket.]

The chantey ceased. But soon a shrill Fragmenter broke out from a new quarter.

"Dionis Coffyn. Hi! Dionis Coffyn's a tomboy."

"Leave the girls be," shouted the gallant Coffin boys.

Dionis walked onward, sedate and unhearing. Surely this particular Dionis Coffyn was not the one meant. Straight shouldered, with her kerchief crossed upon her thin little chest, her gray bonnet hiding her face, her gray skirts moving voluminously forward. There, in the riotous spring sunshine, she was a very spirit of quiet and serenity.

"Tomboy! tomboy!" came the cry again.

Dionis gripped Hopestill's hand.

"Does thee suppose Bob Merrill saw me climb that fence?"

"What if he did?" whispered the loyal Hopestill. "Thee had to climb to get out of the meadow."

"But I climbed worse than that." (A confession, this.) "In Grandmother Severance's garden. That tree with red blossoms. I climbed to the very top. My dress kept catching and tore in three places. I had to dip candles all next day for punishment. I hate to make candles."

"I always make the candles," said Hopestill, a trifle loftily. "I know it tires Mother, so I make them."

Hopestill was a pious child. Her parents never had to command her, she obeyed before the command. Dionis tossed her head.

"I hate candles," she said. "I don't have incomes of the Spirit like thee."

"Oh, don't say that, Dencey. Thee must have the Spirit. The Lord won't wait for thee always. Aunt Vesta said so last meeting." There was tragedy curiously mature in

Hopestill's pleading.

But suddenly the Fragment boys were at their very heels. They had followed the girls up Fair Street and now began anew.

"Hi, Hopestill! Hi, Hopestill! Does yer hope keep still or does it cry out? Oh, I know what she hopes for—a sweetheart. Hope still for a sweetheart."

Dionis, with a swift dip, picked up a stone—a skilled gesture. Her face flushed crimson. Hopestill clutched the uplifted arm.

"Don't, don't thee throw at them. I don't care what they say!"

"Thee should care. I won't have them naming thee in the street."

"Please, Dencey, thee will be sorry."

Dionis struggled in the clasp, but Hopestill held on. "Remember what the discipline says, Dencey. Resist not evil."

It is a wonder with such preachment that Dionis did not break away forthwith. But she loved Hopestill with an adoring love. She dropped the stone and the two walked on, not hastening their pace, apparently serene. Real Quaker self-control.

At their heels kept their tormenters.

"Is it for Bob Merrill ye are hopin' still? Is it for Blake Folger? Who is it, Hopestill?"

Onward steadily. Only the quivering of the rear frills of their drab bonnets showed their mental agony.

Strange cruelty of children!

At the corner of the lane came an unexpected diversion—a rescue, so it seemed at first—for out of the lane came a ragged boy, a boy neither Fragment nor Coffin, who was the peculiar object of all teasing in Nantucket. This boy tempted Fate—*"Whom the gods would destroy they first make mad"*—and he yelled out:

"Oh, you Fragmenters! Goin' to Fragment School! I don't have to go—nowheres."

Instantly the Fragmenters forgot their girl victims.

"Hi! Jetsam, Jetsam," they yelled. "Saved off a wreck like a ole piece o' wood. Driftwood Sammie!"

They referred to the boy's origin. He had been saved from a wreck on the South Shore.

The boy stopped short. His hard little face whitened with anger.

"You—you—you—" he muttered. He seemed vainly trying to think of some retort as brilliant as theirs. His roving eyes met Dionis Coffyn's.

Perhaps he thought Dionis was one of his tormenters. Perhaps he had not the courage to face the Fragment boys. Whatever the cause, he shrilled out at Dencey:

"Hello, Darkie! Portugee girl! Portugee girl!"

Ah, that thorn in the flesh of Dionis Coffyn! No one, not even Hopestill, knew the deep wounding of that thorn—her swarthy complexion. The Coffyns, those that spelled it with a *y*, were dark; and on her mother's side she was related to the Pratts, who some of them "really might be taken for foreigners." The two darknesses had descended together upon Dionis, who was uncompromisingly brunette.

What a fate for a girl!

Suddenly, like a bursting dam, Dencey's long-held self-control gave way. Mob spirit seized her.

The boy Jetsam, with that "Darkie" taunt, had fled, and, with one leap, Dionis was after him. The Fragmenters, too, gave chase—a yelling, shrilling mob. Dionis was in their midst, nay, in the forefront of them, like a flying cloud—all after the same desperate quarry—the Jetsam boy. The housewives of Fair Street hurried to their windows in consternation at the noise. "Those Fragment boys must surely be dealt with."

Dionis ran like a deer, spite of the stays which held her in their whalebone armor, spite of the full, long skirts. It took genius to run with such handicaps. Now she swooped up a stone, threw it forcefully overhand. Heaven only knows where she got her skill. Her dress fluttered balloon-like in the wind, her bonnet fell back, showing the black, black tossing of her hair, her eyes were full of cruel light. She was quite unconscious of the Fragment boys about her. She only knew that Jetsam had called her that terrible name. Now they were out beyond the streets, beyond the lanes. They passed Mill Hill and were flying along the open road in the Commons where Jetsam's home was. He dropped his basket of eggs, a devastating breakage. And still the screaming rout kept after him.

Then a stone—could it have been Dencey's?—hit the boy's shoulder, cut deep, and, with a cry of dismay and of giving up, Jetsam dropped in the road. There he crouched, swaying to and fro, clutching his bleeding shoulder.

"Oh, now ye've done it! Darn ye, darn every one of ye!" he cried. "All right, I'll tell the tithing man on ye. He'll fix ye."

Meanwhile, back in pretty Fair Street, stood Hopestill, clasping her hands together in convulsive horror. She gazed after the disappearing Dionis—the flying disgrace of her, the impossible disaster. In Hopestill's gentle face there was no boasting now, only pity, deep brooding pity.

"Oh, poor Dencey! Why did thee do it!" she moaned, "Oh, thee will be so sorry, so sorry!"

2. *The Consequence Begins*

B UT IN THE calm soul of Hopestill there could be no realization of the sorrow which she prophesied. It was Dencey's sorrow. It came down upon Dencey like the sudden night—a black remorse in which she saw with swift mature judgment the thing she had done. The pitiful thin shoulder blade of the boy bleeding where her missile had cut—she glimpsed it through a rent in his shirt, and how it moved convulsively as with sobs. The boy all of a sudden had given up the fight, he who had been so brave and defiant at the first.

All this brought the dire, overwhelming knowledge to Dionis.

The Fragment boys were swarming about the prone figure. They were a little afraid of what they had done, and this made them the more cruel.

"Aw, git up. Ye ain't hurted. Ye're just monkeyin', ye are."

Dionis dashed in between them like an avenging fury.

"He is hurt," she shouted. "Can't you all see the bleeding? You boys leave him be. Don't you dare touch him!"

"Touch! Lord A'mighty! It was you hit him, not us," laughed the foremost boy.

"Well, anyway, thee leave him alone. You've all done enough. I'll tell the tithing man myself—on all of us, thee, me—all," she cried.

"Well, what do you think of that?" grinned the boy, edging nearer.

Dionis was half sobbing, but there was no weakness in her sobs.

"You get away—every one of you! Go off! Go away!" she stormed. And with a dash wholly unexpected, she flung herself upon the foremost Fragment boy sprawling him backward against the others.

But it was her frenzy which scared them rather than her onslaught. She had summoned some unused and un- expected strength. The Fragmenters fled before it—deri- sive still, but they fled.

Dionis knelt by the boy.

"Oh, I hurt thee! 'Twas me—me that did it."

She snatched out her handkerchief to wipe the wound, but the boy kicked at her viciously. And now he began to launch a string of abusive words which Dionis had never heard before—all at her, all about her. She did not know what the words meant, but somehow they frightened her worse than the blows. They were like some horrible stench she could not bear.

"Don't, oh, don't," she pleaded. "I'm trying—Oh, doesn't thee see I'm sorry? I didn't mean to—"

"Didn't mean to! Good Lord, ye aimed well enough, ye Quaker cat—ye spitfire—ye—ye—ye—"

The boy drowned her words with his swearing and abuse. He leaped up clawing at her. Terror surmounted

Dencey's pity. She struggled to her feet, she turned and ran—ran as though fiends pursued her.

Back toward town along the sandy road—stumbling among the bayberry bushes and over the soft barren heath. Now the first straggling lanes and low houses. She was sobbing, trying to hush her sobs and failing miserably. She could not go to her school, in her disheveled state—into that Quaker neatness. Oh, never. And she must keep still; people would hear her and ask her why. She turned down toward the harbor, threading the streets of the Portuguese, Negroes, and Indian half-breeds—places she hardly knew by sight.

Now she came to the busy shipping district, the low land at the water's edge. The place swarmed with men—such dark-skinned men—rolling barrels, driving drays, drying nets. There was a Fiji Islander in his native costume, or lack of it, nonchalantly busy with the rest. Dionis felt as strange as though she were in some foreign land. Here were the sail lofts, the long narrow sheds of rope walks, the candle factory, and the insistent smell of whale oil. Of course, she was never allowed to come here. Oh, dear, what would Mother say! How one sin led to another and another! What a desperate world!

She must get home, but she must find her way where no one knew her or cared. The absorption in this task quelled her sobs. She straightened her bonnet and tucked in all her hair, smoothed her kerchief and shook out her skirts and again began to go very fast. She could turn now along the harbor edge toward home. Here, streets there were none, only muddy, winding lanes between warehouses. A ship was at the dock, fitting out for her four-year voyage. She was like a busy ant hill toward which all were tending. A delicious smell of pilot-biscuit filled the air. But Dionis noticed none of this. She was terrified at passing the foot of State Street, where surely some uncle or cousin would sight her. She dodged hither and yon behind fish houses and sheds.

Ah, there was Brant Point Light! Home was near. She had only to cross a lonely, sandy place. Desperately, she hurried through the low meadow grass to her own back yard. All the while, she was strangely occupied in pushing something back out of her mind. She was more frightened at this thing within than at any outward adventure. Cautiously, she peered through the high back gate. Only the cow in her yard switched her tail in mild recognition. And Dionis, with heart in her throat, slipped through the yard into the side door and up the back stairs.

Oh, the refuge at last, the deep-fetched breath of relief! She was in her own dormered room.

3. *The Upper Room*

DIONIS CLOSED THE door softly. The vacancy of the room met her, appalling—the view of the wide, dreaming sea from the open windows—appalling too. Oh, better to be out among the harbor streets trying to find her anxious way. Better to have been caught there than this. For here she would have to face it—the thing she had done. The cruel, terrible, unbelievable thing.

She busied herself nervously, untied her bonnet, hung it on its accustomed peg. She was not thinking of God. It was enough that she would have to face herself. She began to brush her hair, but abruptly abandoned it. Slowly she drew from underneath the bed a low stool and sat down upon it and carefully spread her large handkerchief on her knee. Then, suddenly, some spirit thing in her gave way—swept her like a tide with the wind behind it. She began to sob in a shaking fashion new in her experience— huddled together on her low stool.

Yes, this wicked deed had sprung upon her out of the air, so unlooked for. But, no, she had done it herself. Of course, she knew that. Herself, herself! The ancient *mea culpa* rolled through her. She had been wicked before, often, but never this wicked. Never had she hurt anything— cat or dog or even a doll. Surely this was the devil's doing, the devil of whom Presbyterian Grandfather had so fearfully told her. Perhaps she belonged to the devil completely. Some people did. Yes, some people who lived in this very street. Perhaps she too was foreordained to hell.

She had cruelly hurt that poor Sammie Jetsam whom all were hurting. She had cut him on the shoulder with a stone, when everybody, everybody was hurting him too. Of course, he had cursed her and hated her. She deserved it. She deserved it all. Dionis was beyond caring for her mother's reproof or her grandfather's probable whipping. She was past everything—far out on a road she had never trod before.

Toward noon, her mother, coming into the room, found her. Lydia Coffyn was frightened at the child's condition.

"Dionis, what is it?" She knelt by the bowed little figure. "Is thee ill? Why is thee not at school?" She held the small shaking hands. "Be quiet," she commanded. "Does thee hear me? Be quiet and answer my questions. Whatever has happened, thee has no right to act this way. Answer me!"

Suddenly Dencey's voice came back—a strange shrill voice unlike her own, as everything was unlike in this black day.

"Oh, I am wicked, wicked. Thee'd better leave me alone, Mother, Thee'll never love me again."

"Child, never say that. What has thee done? Tell me quickly."

Lydia's fright made her very stern. She actually shook

Dencey's shoulder—a thing unheard of for her to do. She seemed to shake the truth out of her daughter, for it came in a torrent.

"I threw a stone at Jetsam—that boy, thee knows lives with old Injun Jill. I hit him on the shoulder and it cut him, and the blood ran. He fell down, Mother. He fell down because I hit him."

Lydia almost uttered an exclamation, that practice so against Quaker discipline. She faltered out:

"But why? What had he done to thee?"

"Nothing, Mother, just nothing." Dionis was in no mood to recount extenuating circumstances. "Oh, all the Fragment boys were hectoring him, and running after, trying to hurt him. And he was so scared. He ran and ran—way past Mill Hill. And I didn't help him, I helped the boys who were hurting him. I—"

"But, why? Why, Dionis, my child? Why did thee do such a wicked thing?"

"Oh—oh, I don't know!" Dencey's head went down again. "It wasn't just one stone, Mother," she insisted. "I threw and threw and threw until I hit him. And all the boys were throwing stones at him too, and I helped them."

Lydia's self-control returned to her.

"Dionis, thy story has no sense at all. It cannot be so that the boy did nothing to thee and yet thee hurt him. Stop telling falsehoods and tell me the truth!"

But to Dionis now it seemed indeed that Jetsam had done nothing. That terrible name he had called her was so slight a thing compared to her own wrong doing. A kind of loyalty to the boy took hold on her. No, he had done nothing, nothing, she insisted.

Lydia patiently took another tack.

"Thee says he fell down, but surely he got up again. Thee did not hurt him so badly as that."

"Yes, Mother, he got up. And, oh, he won't forgive me. He'll never forgive me. But he shouldn't anyway—no, no!"

"Dionis, why is thee so extravagant? Of course he should forgive thee if thee asked him."

"Yes, I asked him. But he can't. He kicked me and hated me." Dionis sat up blinking. "I'm glad he kicked me, I wish he had kicked me worse."

"Dionis Coffyn," said her mother with great solemnity, "listen to me. Forgiveness is not with that boy. It is not with me, nor even with Grandfather. Thee knows—surely thee knows—forgiveness is with God."

Dionis looked up shrinking.

"Lay thy sin before the Lord. He will forgive and not another. Will thee do that, Dionis, at once? I will leave thee alone here."

Ah, it was upon her again. That busy invisible world which impinged so close upon New England life—the world of heaven and the spirit. Some minds close like a trap at a problem of mathematics. Dionis's mind closed upon these religious phrases which were in everyone's mouth. "Lay thy sin before the Lord," "Enter into the Silence," "Follow the Light."

What did it all mean? She could not even form questions about them, much less experience them. They were all one foggy puzzle, but she was expected to understand these experiences. Every New England child was expected to understand them.

Dencey's uplifted face showed only daunting.

"Now, Dionis, I will not have thee obstinate."

Lydia thought enviously of her sister's child, Hopestill,

who never gave one hour of religious anxiety. "Mother is pleading with thee. Lay thy sin before the Lord—yes, before it is too late."

"But I don't want—" Dionis began, but sharply closed her lips upon the sacrilege.

"What was thee about to say?" demanded Lydia. "Tell me. Speak out."

"I can't, Mother."

"Obey me at once!"

"I don't want God to forgive me. I want that boy to forgive me. I didn't hit God with a stone."

"Thee did. That's just the point, Dionis, thee did."

But, as Lydia was speaking, a Bible phrase "was opened to her," as so often happened with those who knew whole books by heart. "First reconcile thyself to thy brother and then . . ." She sighed with puzzlement.

"Perhaps thee is right. Thee says such strange things sometimes. There—I will take thee to the boy myself, and thee shall ask him. Then will thee pray? Will thee?"

Dionis leaped to her feet, almost forgetting to answer. How her dark little face could change in a moment!

"Yes, yes!" But while she was saying it, she was already running to the press and taking out her bonnet. Lydia could not but be touched at her eagerness. After all, it was only forgiveness the child wanted. Lydia had not intended to go so promptly, but—

"I will get my bonnet too," she said kindly. She turned toward the door, but that moment it was burst open by the little maid, Peggy Runnel.

"Oh, Lydia, come quick!" she cried. (Titles of respect were absent from Quaker address.) "Martha White's been took somethin' awful, an' they're hollerin' over the side fence for thee to come."

"But she was well—a half hour ago. I saw—"

"But—but"—stammered Peggy, tripping over her tongue with news—"the crier's been callin' out on State Street that the *Rachel's* sighted. An' John, he come runnin' home an' took the spyglass, an' run up to the Walk, he did. An' he seen her right off close to the bar, an' her flag at half mast. An' what does John do, he comes runnin' down an' calls to his mother, 'The *Rachel's* in an' her flag half mast.' And Martha, she just says, 'It's Henry,' an' p'r'aps it is, too, sence he's capting. An' they can't git her outen her faint."

Lydia was pale, for she loved Martha White. But her manner was not unquieted; it was, however, swift. "Dionis, I am sorry, I cannot go now."

"Oh—oh." Dionis dared not voice her disappointment save in this breathless word. Even Dionis hardly ever answered back, it simply was not done.

Now the ringing bell, the long sonorous call of the crier came up from the street, "The brig *Rachel*. Just behind the bar. Flag half mast!" and the running feet along the street.

"Has thee no pity for Martha?" said Lydia, shocked.

But Dionis snatched off her bonnet with little grace. As she did so, her black mane of hair came tumbling down about her face. She glimpsed it in the mirror, a startling sight, and with it the old bitter questions flashed unbidden to her tongue.

"Mother, why is my face so dark? Am I adopted and not thy very own? Did thee get me off a Portugee ship, Mother?"

Lydia was struck dumb! The frivolousness of it, the

heartlessness of such a question at this time. She flushed deep with anger, stood with compressed lips until the flush faded. Then she spoke:

"Dionis, I believe thee has been mocking me all this while. Now, go to thy bed at once. And stay there without dinner. Grandfather shall punish thee. I must find some way to teach thee to be less heartless and wicked than thee is."

Then the door closed and Dionis was alone with her sins.

4. *Forgiveness for the Stone*

L YDIA DID NOT easily forget a promise. But the events of the next few days were all-absorbing.

The mourning flag was indeed for Captain Henry White, who had perished miserably of a fever off the coast of Chili. Martha White was very quiet, saying not a word, but strangely refusing to rise from her chair. She sat gazing into space with a questioning horror into which no friend could break. Her little son Henry, born since his father's departure, sat in her lap, seeming to understand by some curious infant cognizance his mother's sorrow. Martha clung to the child with a desperate clinging. Only when tending him did her face lighten a little from its gloom. Then the babe sickened. Lydia helped nurse him night and day. But he slipped away from their arms.

"God took him 'cause He saw it was something for me to love," said Martha, and no persuasion could make her recede from this.

Then Martha too fell ill.

Martha White's suffering cut Lydia to the heart. No hours were too many to devote to her. Day and night she kept by her side. No one but Lydia could make the patient take her slender meals. No one but Lydia could break up the long hours of restlessness and suffering and quiet her to sleep.

Meanwhile, Dionis lived through the endless day in her room, lived through her grandfather's labored reproof and switching, and worst of all, the return to school. The event of Captain White's death and his widow's sorrow were all outside her consciousness. It is hard to realize how dim is grief to the child who has never known it. Dionis was not allowed to go into Martha White's chamber. Indeed, would have shrunk from it, in any case. Besides, her own deed and wickedness covered her whole horizon. All life was changed and the aspect of it.

On her walks to school she looked anxiously up street and lane for the boy Jetsam. Heretofore, she had often met him, but now he came no more. Perhaps he was dead. That picture of him crouching on the ground clutching his bleeding shoulder repeated itself again and again in her mind. Sometimes it awoke her at night, sometimes passed cloud-like between her and her spelling book. And sometimes the picture evolved others.

She saw him laid out wrapped in a white shroud. She had seen Martha White's little Henry lying that way—so quiet, so strangely removed, though near. Now she followed Jetsam to his grave. Then, as often as not, resurrected him to go through the story in a different way.

"What is thee thinking of?" Hopestill would query. "I've asked thee a question twice, and thee doesn't answer."

No, for had she not been at Jetsam's bedside holding his hand? Already he was quite changed—a saintly and beautiful Jetsam, who said solemnly, "I forgive thee,

Dencey Coffyn. I forgive thee." And he would let no one smooth his pillow and bring him a cup of water but Dencey. She was like her mother at Mrs. White's bedside, necessary, beloved, waited-for.

Then upon these glowing imaginings burst the plan—the clearing, dream-shattering plan.

She would go out to Injun Jill's cottage and find Jetsam—not in dream but in actuality. With her own proper voice she would ask his forgiveness and get it. Mother was too busy to go. By the same token, Mother would not notice her absence. The thing did not bear delay.

Real adventure was here, palpitating, absorbing. It led her on like a half-told tale. The going must be secret. After school was the best time. Instead of coming home, she could go to Aunt Lovesta's and from there to Injun Jill's. Injun Jill's cottage was out on the Commons near Rotten Pumpkin Pond. Dionis had glimpsed it from afar, when she went to Farmer Brown's. It was not a near nor an easy place. So much the better!

And she must take with her some atoning gift. She had lamed Jetsam for life—she was sure of that much. What gift could make that even? In her room was a sea trunk which had belonged to Grandfather. Children of sailors inherit such cast-off romance. The little hairy calfskin thing which had traveled three oceans, escaping by hand's-breadth from pirate and shipwreck, now held the treasure gatherings of a little girl.

There was a humming bird which by some miracle did not smell, but had wind-dried. If you turned it about, its neck was now a solemn deepening blue and now a startling fire—marvelous, and so tenderly small. There was a tarantula's nest from Brazil, which looked like a lump of clay, but had a tiny hinged door which revealed within a pure white room.

Then there was the ammonite.

Dionis, leaning over her treasures, picked this up and held it in a caressing palm. Father had brought her this all the way from some South Pacific island. He had slit it in halves, showing all the chambers within. "The Chambered Nautilus" had not yet been written, but the shell needed no human interpreter to speak the poetic act which it held in form. The outside was engraved with a flower. Father always made flowers on his scrimshont work:

She gazed at the ammonite a moment. The most precious thing of all. Then she laid it in her lunch basket. Yes, she would take that.

Then she went to school.

Oh, the length of that day at school! Debby, the teacher, must have known that Dionis was planning something wicked. For, every time she looked up, Debby's eye was upon her. And Dionis spelt *concentration* with *sh* and *conscience* with a *k*. Of course, Debby rapped her knuckles for that. Even helping the little ones was no joy to-day. The school was run on the new Lancastrian plan, and, young as she was, Dionis had yet younger children to care for and instruct. She had brought her only book, *Pilgrim's Progress*, to show the children, and let them spell the littlest words. But she could not interest them to-day. At lunch hour she could eat nothing for excitement.

At last the last lesson was said, the last sum added, and the class stood in a circle in the middle of the floor. Clara Gardner shifted her feet, Bobby coughed, then choked it, Sally giggled and clapped her hand over her mouth. Debby, the teacher, stood resting her hands together, as she always did, grimly waiting. At last all sounds died into an utter, utter silence. Then Hopestill, who had been the best child for the day, lifted her hand high and let drop a pin!

It struck the bare floor and was heard. "So still you could hear a pin drop." That was the necessity.

Then clatter, clatter of stout little copper-toed shoes, finding of bonnets and hats, pinning on of shawls, and Dionis was free.

5. *Out on the Commons*

DIONIS SPED ALONG the narrow lanes. What a sense of freedom—flying toward a goal.

She would find Jetsam at last, get his forgiveness. That awful sense of anger against herself—she would dispel it now.

There on the hill, the four clattering windmills gestured against the sky. Only one of them was not working, because the miller was "turning it into the wind," swinging around the whole top of it by means of the down-stretched spar which the weary old horse was dragging. They were almost like ships, these mills.

She passed Mill Hill and stepped at once into the clean, open heart of the world.

The Commons swept away grandly from the place of her feet. Hollows flowed down into reverent shadow, heights lifted themselves in softening distances, and beyond all a glimpse of intense blue showed the circle of the sea. Dionis caught her breath. Her thoughts became light and drifted out into space. A good fortune was Dencey's. Whatever gloom might invade her from without, the ways

25

of her mind were ways of pleasantness. She hurried forward on the rut-road. To-day was a "dry northeaster," the clearest weather in Nantucket. Far out on the plains were little white tufts of thistledown. Those were the sheep, hundreds and hundreds of them that had to be sheared in the spring when they had the Shearing Festival. In the distance was a toy house so small she could put it in her basket, a magic thing which only people tiny as birds could live in. But as Dionis trudged and trudged the house suddenly swelled life-size, and she had to acknowledge that it was Farmer Brown's.

Gracious—where was she? Dionis suddenly came back to earth with her dreams in shreds. She was all alone and the wide Commons about her everywhere. Here in the silence they seemed to have a mood like a thoughtful yet sleeping face.

Dencey gazed about her. Far over to the right, half submerged by the flowing lines of hills, she saw Injun Jill's cottage. Dencey's sombre mission came back—a flip of bat's wings.

She was afraid of Injun Jill. Every child in the school was afraid of her, and ran from her in the streets. But how much better to meet her in the street than out here in this wide loneliness. The boys said she was a witch, and Dionis tried not to believe it. And Jetsam! Oh, why had she ever thought he would forgive her? Hadn't he kicked her and sworn at her and done nothing else?

Her unwilling feet dragged and dragged her closer to the cabin. Now it stood out, bare and dismal. Oh, if she only had some shelter. Why, she could be seen for miles. And what if Injun Jill came out! Only an enormous purpose kept her going. But at the outskirts of the place she stopped. She could not make herself knock at the door. Jetsam must be in there, lying on his bed. Maybe he was unconscious. How dead the windows looked, and how gruesome Rotten Pumpkin Pond beside the house.

Suddenly the wide silence was broken by a sound—blanketed in distance, chop, chop, chop! There was a rise beyond the house. Someone was chopping on the farther side of it. With pounding heart, Dionis passed the house and climbed the hilltop. In the hollow below was a stretch of scrub pine. The little tortured trees were sheared atop as level as a hedge. Thus high could they grow in the hill's protection; then the sharp sea winds sheared them.

The chopping was there. Perhaps the woodman would help her and take her to Injun Jill.

Soft as a cat, Dencey crept down to the woods, peered in, and saw—

Not a man at all, but Jetsam himself, erect on his feet, alive and well. Some Power better than her own had brought all her evil to naught. A warm radiance swept Dencey. She stood looking from her covert at the comforting sight.

He was felling one of the trees, the wounded shoulder doing its part with health and precision. He was whistling a gay but tuneless whistle. How dirty his shirt was. The very same shirt Dencey had seen before, the very same rents and tears.

Beside him, among the chips, a dog sat gazing up at him.

Suddenly this dog wheeled, bristling on all fours, then sprang like a bolt into the thicket and upon Dencey. She screamed with terror, clutching her basket in front of her, for the dog's paws were on her chest.

The boy banged down his ax and came running.

"Hey, Wash! Down I say!"

He seized the dog by the neck, pulling and struggling. Then he was aware of Dionis.

"Tarnation to it! If it ain't that little she-divil agin. What ye doin' hyar?"

Dionis was utterly speechless. She hadn't her breath yet, anyway. And to explain her sacred errand was impossible in this confusion.

"Whad ye want?" demanded Jetsam, threatening. "Throw some more stones, will ye, will ye?"

"Oh, no, no. I came—I came—"

"I'll show ye. Slippin' up on me like a doggone thief!"

The intrusion of her coming at all broke upon Dionis with profound embarrassment. As for Jetsam, he was piqued for his woodland skill. No woodsman save a dead one would have let an intruder come so close.

"Did ye come to see Injun Jill?"

"No, to see thee."

"Don't ye go to thee'in' me. I kin knock ye down if I wantter."

This ungallant deed was prevented by Wash. He broke away from his master with little short yelps.

"Come back, darn ye!" quoth the boy irritably. "Ye don't hev to be chawin' up an spittin' out everybody what comes."

But the dog pawed the basket, wiggling his nose.

"Ye've got meat in that thar, I reckon," said Jetsam. "Wash hain't hed no meat, not fer a month. Tain't right fer a dog, eatin' apples an' sich. He'll lose his stren'th."

Jetsam seemed voicing some old grievance.

"But I have got meat," exclaimed Dionis. "Wash can have it."

She fished busily in her basket and held out the meat. Wash swallowed it at one gulp—almost her hand as well.

The dog was pleased, but the boy was crosser than ever.

"That thar hain't fittin' fer a dog," he complained. "That was human vittles. Roast lamb. What ye gin him that fer?"

"I—I thought thee wanted me to," whimpered Dionis.

Irritability was so unknown to her well-ordered home that it was both surprising and painful.

"I've got some pie," she ventured. "It's mince." For Peggy, that morning, no doubt, instructed by some god, had filled Dencey's basket to the brim.

Jetsam's eyes glittered. He swallowed hard.

"I don't want yer pie. I hain't no beggar," he said.

"But Injun Jill begs for thee," said the downright Quakeress.

"She don't nuther. She's been drunk, anyway, fer a week."

"But she gets your dinner just the same, doesn't she?" Whoever heard of the daily routine of the household being broken?

"No, she don't—lying thar in bed like a ole hawg. Anyways, drunk or sober, her cookin's a cussed mess."

The resentment, the loathing of the whole week were in Jetsam's tone. Again Dionis recoiled. But had she come on this far adventure to be beaten by a swear? I trow not!

"I'll tell thee," she said brightly. "I'll eat one bite and thee eat the next."

She lifted out the pie, all flaky crust and black plumminess. She daintily bit off the nose of the wedge and handed it. Jetsam took one huge bite, then another— and another with hasty gulps. Dionis was taken aback. In her set, the sacred alternation once promised was strictly adhered to.

"Thee eats just as bad as Wash," she commented.

"I don't nuther. Anyways, eatin's eatin', hain't it?"

"No, it isn't. If we should eat like cats and dogs, pretty soon we'd be 'em!"

This bit of evolutionary wisdom was from Peggy.

The boy's face glowered. Quaker truth-telling is often trying.

Oh, dear, she had made him angry again, and she was no nearer asking him to forgive her than she had been in the first place. Could she say it now—just bare and flat out? She hid her face, pretending to look in her basket. Oho!—she had forgotten the ammonite. She took it out reverently. Her voice was soft.

"I—I want to give thee this."

"What, now! Oh, I can't eat that."

Dionis laughed at this sally.

"No, but look," she turned the enchased surface with its white veil-thin flower on the pink background, a true shell cameo. Pride was in her gesture.

"Father carved it just for me. It's a flower he found in Callao. First he made a picture of it in the log book, so as to get it accurate." (A fine word that though quoted.) "For it's a Holy Ghost flower. See the dove in the center?"

Jetsam stared. "Wha'd I do with it?" he demanded.

"Keep it. It's beautiful."

"But hit's just a shell. Shells hain't no good. Even the sea spits 'em out all over the beaches."

Was Dencey going to fail after all?

"Oh, but this one—just look." In a kind of desperation, Dionis forced the shell into his dirty hands.

"I don't want it, I tell ye," he said. "Say, what's the matter with ye, anyway?"

"I—I want thee—" Dionis faltered at the word—"to forgive me."

"Forgive?" he seemed scarcely to understand the word. "What fer?"

"For hitting thee with—with that stone."

The angry memory rushed back into the boy's face.

"I guess ye won't pay fur that with no durned shell," he said. "Thar!"

And he flung the ammonite hard against a tree, where it broke into fragments.

"Oh—oh—oh!"

Dionis cried out as if he had broken herself. She dashed after the shell, picking up the pieces with cold fumbling fingers. She was too amazed to cry, too horrified for anger. It couldn't be vanished, this thing she had treasured for years. Jetsam viewed her with fine indifference.

"I'll pay ye fur hittin' me in the street," he swaggered. "A girl. I reckon no girl'll hit *me* agin."

But Dionis did not hear him. She was putting the delicate fragments back into her basket. To find place for them, she took out all her books.

At sight of the books, the boy leaned forward in tense eagerness. He reached out his hands. *Webster's Spelling Book, Young Ladies' Accidence*—he went hastily through these, fluttering the leaves. Then *Pilgrim's Progress*. At this he paused, bending over it, closely gazing at the picture of Pilgrim and his burden. Then he looked up. An expression of eerie cunning crossed his face, made it almost pixy-like.

"Gimme this!" he said sharply. "Ef ye're so crazy to gimme suthin', gimme this hyar book."

Dencey turned and gasped. Her *Pilgrim's Progress*—the one and only book that was her very own. This was so intimate a thing that giving it had not occurred to her.

"Not—not that one," she faltered.

But the sense of her wrong-doing was strong upon her. She must pay—must pay. She had known that from the beginning. Had she not heard of the "wages of sin"?

"Yes," she answered breathlessly. "Thee can have it." But at the words something caught her throat with terrible pain.

Jetsam sat bending over the book, turning the leaves, not pausing at any, with the busy curiosity of a monkey. He had not even thanked her. To Dionis, the whole situation became suddenly sordid. Jetsam and his dirty, dirty shirt, Jetsam and the cabin over the hill, where Injun Jill lay drunk "like a hawg." She had come out to ask for forgiveness, but Jetsam had only broken her ammonite, and now had snatched from her her precious *Pilgrim's Progress*. And he was hating her while he read it. Hating—hating still.

"I guess I should have asked God after all," she muttered.

Jetsam peered up.

"What ye cryin' fur?" he demanded.

"I'm not cryin', I'm breathin'," she answered.

"Ye air cryin' too. Say, looky hyar. Ef ye like yer book so much, why did ye give it to me?"

"Be—because I hurt thee."

"Huh!" he grunted. "Ye think yerself awful smart, hurtin' folks."

She didn't. She did not think herself smart. But how was she to tell him? In a kind of blankness, Dionis lifted her basket and slowly went back along the path over the hill.

6. *The Price of Forgiveness*

DIONIS STUMBLED ALONG, frankly crying. Strange how much longer the way seemed now. The wind had changed. The sky had dimmed, and all the hills and hollows gone gray. She wished the path were plainer. Here, where the barren heath was so thick a carpet, there was no path at all. Thee had to trace it as best thee could, there on the farther rise. What if she got lost! She had a deep sense of the ugliness she had seen, a strange intimation, such as sometimes comes to children, of the cruelty of the world which is yet all unknown, all to be lived through.

She had gone a good way when, suddenly, she stopped to listen. Something, yes, steps following her. She began to run, but the steps gained. They were running too. At last, for very terror, she looked around.

It was Jetsam. Oh, what would he do to her now! But, try as she might, he was soon up with her.

"Hyar," he said, thrusting at her her precious *Pilgrim's Progress*. "Take it. I don't want it. It hain't no good to me."

33

But Dionis was not one who, having put hand to the plow, looketh back. The sacrifice was completed. It was not for naught that she had an ancestress who had been whipped at a cart's-tail through three towns to make her recant. She pushed the book from her.

"It's thine now."

"Hit's no good to me. I tell ye, I can't make no head nor tail o' the thing." There was no kindness in the giving back, a furious bafflement, rather, which Dionis did not understand.

"I won't take it, so there," she said, hurrying away.

But Jetsam still walked with her—that is, abreast of her, on the other side of the rut-road, silently, doggedly. Dionis glanced over at him in puzzlement, and still they went on.

The pretty town came into sight, etched on the horizon like a picture, the windmills wheeling against the sky, the golden-topped tower which always looks brightest against a gray sky.

Suddenly Jetsam broke silence.

"Kin ye read?"

"Of course I can. Ever since before Father went away."

"I spose ye spells the letters and then says the words," he ventured.

"I do not. I read like talking—straight along. I'm not a baby."

Quickly Jetsam crossed the road, opening the book as he came.

"Then read it," he demanded. "Thar. Read it right thar."

The book had fallen open at a habitual page. Dionis looked down. " 'So Pilgrim went on and Apollyon met him.' "

Dencey's fancy took fire at the words. She could never read this page without chills of fear and shivers of delight.

" ' "Whence come you and whither are you bound?" ' "

She read the fiend's question with all the direfulness that was in it.

Then her voice rang out the answer.

" ' "I come from the City of Destruction, and I am going to the City of Zion." ' "

On she went through the terrible battle, man against foul fiend. She hardly knew she was reading. It was reality. Dencey's bonnet nodded the rhythm, for she knew it like a song. They stood close together, these two children of stern old New England, absorbed in New England's book of Power.

" 'Then Apollyon straddled quite over the whole breadth of the way, and said, "Prepare thyself to die, for I swear, by my infernal den—Here I will spill thy soul." ' "

"Lordy—he's a goner," breathed Jetsam.

But Dionis was quite unconscious of Jetsam. She read on to the victory:

" 'And Christian made at him again, saying, "Nay, in all these things we are more than conquerors Romans seven thirty-seven." And with that Apollyon spread forth his dragon wings and sped him away James four seven.' "

Bible references and all she read in the same triumphant voice, and handed the book back to its owner. Jetsam crossed over to the other side of the road and without a word began his steady forward tramp.

"Humph!" Dionis heard him grunt, Indian-like. "Humph!" The admiration was patent, and Dionis began to glow. But at the third "humph" the boy stopped. His chin went down on his chest. His whole body drooped.

"I kain't read," he blurted out. "Not a durned word."

The shame of the confession showed in every line of him. Dionis felt shamed too, as if, somehow, she were to blame. It couldn't be that this great boy, as big as she, could not read. She felt as she did that day when she found stern old Grandfather sobbing over Henry White's death.

These things were most upsetting.

"But thee can learn," she said hastily. "Thee has the book now."

"Not the way ye kin," was the wrathful response.

Dionis crossed over to him and opened the book again. "Look," she said. "The *i*'s always have dots and the *t*'s are crossed like that and the *o*'s are round like a hoople. And that, right there," she pointed with her slender brown finger—"is Apollyon. Now thee knows three letters and one word."

He stood peering close at the book, then in despair:

"I kain't do it. I kain't. I tried out thar hard, and I kain't."

An intense desire took hold of Dionis to fix all this.

"I could teach thee," she said. "Yes, I could."

"Teach me!" he repeated. "Larn me to read? Ye?" He looked at her without the least hope.

"Yes, I teach the little ones in school."

"But would yer mother let ye?" he inquired.

Here was a stunner. No self-respecting mother in Nantucket would let her child associate with Sammie Jetsam—especially a girl.

Jetsam himself answered. "No, she wouldn't, she wouldn't."

Still he stood there.

"But ye could," he asserted suddenly. "Ye could do it.

Hit would take a long while, but ye could. Look hyar," he added abruptly, "I hain't forgive ye yet."

"Dear me!" Dionis had forgotten all about forgiveness. It came back with a pang.

"But, looky hyar, you gal. Ef ye teach me to read I will forgive ye. I will. Not afore, mind ye. Not afore, but when I kin read like you kin."

"But I'm the best reader in the whole school."

"All right, then. Not quite so good as ye read, but good enough. Will ye do it?"

She hesitated. The difficulties were enormous. What would Mother say? Dared she disobey?

"All right, then," said Jetsam bitterly. "I won't forgive ye."

"Yes, I'll do it," she promised.

"Cross yer heart and double D?"

"I don't make vain oaths, Sam Jetsam, but I will."

He searched her face.

"When will ye begin? To-morrow?"

"After school, I can," she breathed anxiously.

"All right. Then ye come out hyar beyond the windmills. Do ye heed me?" He began to plan with sudden animation. "Do ye see that thar little pine and then further out Brown's house?"

"Yes," she said, wondering.

"Well, ye walk along this hyar road until that pine tree comes right front o' Brown's house. Then ye've got yer bearin's and stop. An' I'll meet ye."

"But suppose it's foggy and I can't see Farmer Brown's."

"Then ye'll have to come by dead reckonin'," he conceded.

"Would the old Walden pig-pen be dead reckonin'?" she queried.

"I guess so. But pig-pens hain't so good as bearin's. Now, don't ye forgit. To-morrow."

Without a word of good-bye, he turned and walked away. His determined little figure trudged into the distance up the farther rise, still clutching his book. Clutching her too, Dionis seemed to feel, as she watched him go. Making her do what he would.

BOOK TWO

7. *The Former Time*

WHEN THE WHITE fire of New England life sprang up along the Massachusetts coast, a spark of it blew far out to sea and became—Nantucket.

Here was to be seen, as in a diminishing glass, a tiny New England, delicately outlined—intensified—in a word, islanded. Here were the New England character and hardihood, its God-fearing and mental eagerness, yet all sensitively changed, individualized, so that they became Nantucket and no other. Instead of the stony fields of New England, the Nantucketers plowed the wide ocean, and at this period of their history, their harvest was gathered from pole to pole. By its industry, this low, sandy island, eighteen miles long, produced enough whale oil to light half the cities of the world, including London.

Clearly defined smallness on the one hand, world wideness on the other, made the Nantucket life different from all others.

The legend of Nantucket's founding is a twice-told tale, but it is so true to the character of the Island as always to need retelling. How Thomas Macey of Salisbury, Massachusetts, gave shelter overnight to three fleeing Quakers, how for this act of humanity he was fined, questioned, and hectored by the Puritan authorities, until the New England in him rose in wrath against New England; and taking an open boat, he, with two others, put out for the small island off the coast. All Puritanism was a protest, but Nantucket was a protest against protest.

Later on, mainly through the inspiration of one powerful woman, Mary Starbuck, Nantucket became almost entirely Quaker. Imagine it, the tiny gray island clothing itself in gray, unafraid of austerity because of the colorful spirit within.

In this little and complete world, the Coffins had lived since 1660. At one time there were five hundred persons of the name of Coffin living on the Island—"not countin' the Coffin family that wa'n't real Coffins"—that line being founded by a Portuguese cabin boy whom a Coffin captain adopted.

Tom Coffyn was, needless to say, of the genuine variety. He spelled his name with a y as did the first Coffyn founder. He it was who afterward was to become Dionis's father. Lydia Severance, afterward her mother, had always lived there, she and her ancestors before her.

Their meeting was at meeting.

To say that they first met there is hardly true, for they had seen each other, as all Island young folk did, at sheep-shearing, at corn-huskings, or passing in the street. But Tom Coffyn was of the First Congregationalist Church and Lydia Severance of the Friends' Meeting on Pleasant Street. So they went to different schools, and the youthful acquaintance was slight. Love at first sight, then, this encounter might be called, a thing not unusual in Nantucket, where happy meetings followed the four-year loneliness of the whaling voyage. From such a voyage Tom Coffyn had just returned when on that First Day morning he chose to go to Quaker meeting with his voyage comrade, Caleb Severance.

Into the gray room filed the gray and silent people, the women on one side, the men on the other, with certain honorable ones facing the meeting from a row of higher benches. The room was perfectly bare save for the candlesticks set at intervals along the walls. The large windows let in all the glare. Only this morning a poplar, golden with autumn, standing outside in the sunlight, threw its glory into the place and filled the gray room with a spell of gold.

Tom did not at all recognize the maiden who seated herself third from the aisle in the fifth row. She must be from Rhode Island or perhaps the "Continent." There she sat among the drab and quiet sisterhood. "Heavens!" thought Tom, "how futile to dress the women all alike when one can shine out from the rest so star-like and distinguished." He must have forgotten in the long four-year glimpses of foreign women how beautiful a woman could be, how wide-set and sweet her gray eyes, how rosy and demure her mouth. In what way Tom managed to see all this across the straight-seated rows is a mystery. But he did so manage.

The Quaker silence began. So many people sitting together not communicating with each by any word, but waiting—waiting for something outside of themselves. There was awe in the silent room. Obedience made visible. Tom could hear the poplar rustling softly in the sea wind. And once a solitary pedestrian passed in the street, was heard from far, coming, and his footsteps persisted a great distance toward town. Still the Quakers sat. Gracious, that girl was beautiful, with her downcast eyes and folded hands. There seemed an actual light in her face. Tom decided that he approved of this Quaker silence. Was there always such happiness in it? he wondered. The Divine love was played upon by a tender human dawning until both were roseate together. Now he saw the girl sway in her seat—ever so slightly, like a flower in a breath of wind. Her hands moved, she blushed slowly red. By Jove, he had been staring. He must stop it.

But the honored ones who faced the meeting knew well the signs of one whom the Spirit moves. Lydia Severance had never spoken in meeting before. A faint stir of expectation could just be felt in the deeps of meditation.

Lydia rose, swaying flower-like as before, her hands, touching the rail in front of her, passed back and forth softly as willow branches touching the grass. Then, startlingly upon the silence, her voice began—an inner voice, nothing earthly about it. Ah, surely she was "in the Spirit."

"I feel drawings in my mind to thank Thee, O Lord, for the return of the *White Wave*. Lord, only Thou didst bring her out of the stormy seas and cruel hurricane. Only Thou didst know the preciousness of her souls to bring them home."

The *White Wave!* Tom's own ship. But this was a miracle. Why on earth was she doing it? What was she saying?

Her speech was not speech but chanting. All of the sentences on one tone save the last word, which dropped strangely to *almost* a tone below. Then, suddenly, a sentence began a delicate third higher, as though some new impulse of the Spirit had sent it up, and slowly drooped again to the original chanting tone. Singing, no less! Exquisite music denied by the rigid creed of their sect, yet finding its way unmarked to their very holy of holies.

And all her chanting was of the *White Wave* and her return from perilous seas.

Tom was lost in wonder. Like a flickering light, her blessings ran from bow to stern of the ship, from keel to masthead. At her touch, the sordid things grew sacred— the filthy ports they had made and escaped from, the storms they had ridden out swearing at the bitter effort, the very whales they had caught—all these were, somehow, in her prayer.

As the meeting broke up with shaking of hands and solemn greetings, Tom pulled his comrade's arm.

"Who is that wonderful girl over there—fifth row?" Why, his voice was actually trembling!

"That one with the brown eyes?" asked Caleb. "Abigail Folger—yes, she's—"

"Heavens, no! The gray-eyed one—the one who spoke."

"Oh, that one! Lydia, my sister."

Even yet, Tom thought the "speech" was for him. "Then I know her," he exclaimed.

Without more word, he shouldered his way across and caught up with her at the door. He put out his hand. The golden poplar was not brighter than his smile.

"Good-morning, Miss Lydia. Do you know who I am?" he asked.

"Yes. Tom Coffyn. But thee didn't know me at first."

"How did you know I didn't? You must have been looking at me in meeting."

The rogue! He was delighted with the confusion this

caused under the Quaker bonnet.

"May I walk home with you?" he pleaded. "I'd like to very much."

"It's quite out of thy way," she began.

"No, it isn't. Your way couldn't be that for me."

Truly a forward youth!

He did not go into her house that day. Sabbaths, or First Days, were not congenial for visiting or pleasures. But the next day he called upon her and stayed to supper, too. The next day and the next he was there. At the husking he sat by Lydia—saw no one else in the barn. He even took her to a quilting party in the middle of the afternoon. He scandalized the Congregationalists by going to Quaker meeting three Sabbaths in succession.

Lydia bloomed like a wild rose under the sudden adoration. Bloomed though she spent many prayerful hours trying to stem the tide that was carrying her along. Marrying out of meeting was the supreme wrong in Quakerism. She would be disowned. The sorrow and disgrace of it would spread through all her kith and kin.

"Lydia," said her mother severely, "how long is thee going to accept the attentions of Lias Coffyn's son? Are there not enough good boys of Friends' Meeting to please thee? Soon I shall have to forbid him the house."

Lydia tried her best. But what could she do? She could not shut the door in Tom's face—that bright and laughing face that seemed to bring very sunshine in with it. And if she went down town on any errand, he was sure to find her and accompany her home. All too soon came the fateful evening.

All the family and friends were invited to Cousin William's, who had just returned from a whaling voyage.

Lydia stayed at home for conscience' sake, knowing that Tom would be there. She had out her spinning wheel and paced before it, holding the outstretched thread in the warm firelight. Oh, she was trying to still her thoughts—trying not to dream so happily—when the big brass knocker knocked on her heart louder than on the door.

Trembling, she opened the door. Of course, it was he.

"You didn't come to the party," he said, as they came into the room. "I'm glad, for I'd rather see you here."

He was scared, too. Mark how his dear hand trembled, holding his hat. Why, she had forgot her manners.

"Will thee give me thy hat?" she ventured, with out-stretched hand. But he dropped his hat, caught her hand in both of his, gazing into her eyes until her soul drew out to his.

And what is he saying? Oh, the dreadful, doomful words, for Lydia cannot marry out of Meeting, throw herself into outer darkness, almost damnation. It would break Mother's heart, and, oh Father's wrath when he comes home from sea! Impossible—impossible!

"Oh, no no!"—Lydia cries it out with horror and shrink-ing. "I can't marry you—I can't."

"You don't love me," said Tom fatally. "I—I never thought you could—an angel like you giving yourself—to me."

He stooped blindly to pick up his hat—his tall best beaver, worn for her sake—even that touched her. He would go now, that was best. Why couldn't she keep still? But he must not go. He must not go away thinking that lie.

"I do love thee, Tom. Oh, Tom, I do."

Then she cannot help it. He has her in his arms, sweeping her into heavenly places and spaces. Oh, surely it is wrong to kiss like that. For she must not marry him. No— no—no!

8. *"I cannot marry out of Meeting"*

AFTER THIS FATEFUL evening, Lydia did not even go abroad on the street. She would not see Tom when he came to the house, and only the severe Mrs. Severance met him at the door. Her brother Caleb was no help.

"Of course, Lydia's all right," he declared. "I don't wonder thee likes her. But she'll never marry out of Meeting—Lydia won't. She's the most pious of all the family."

Tom was desparate. Ten days passed, and he did not even see her face. He was sure Mrs. Severance took his letters, for he received no answers. Darkness settled on his soul. He was sure he would die.

Mrs. Severance, looking out at the side window, said, with exasperation:

"There's that Coffyn boy going by again. I should think he'd be ashamed. He looks as though he were condemned to the gallows."

And Lydia tangled her thread on the distaff—tried and tried to untangle it. But who can untangle a thread through blinding tears?

She even stayed home from meeting, for her headaches were not feigned. Sorrow and imprisonment are not healthful exercises. But she had to go into the garden for the vegetables, and one day, Tom, passing along the fenced lane, saw her among the pumpkin vines. He leaped over the high fence at a bound. He had not climbed the shrouds on the high seas for naught.

Lydia stopped, rooted to the spot, holding the pumpkin like a full moon in her arms.

"Lydia, how could you!" he cried. "How could you hide from me!"

For a moment she could not speak. To see him again! It somehow made such a commotion, such a glare of happiness.

"I don't dare," she whispered. "Oh, Tom, if I see thee, I—I—"

"Lydia, I couldn't throw you over for anything. What if I am a Congregationalist? I'd love you if you were a Fiji— if you were a—a—oh, heaven, I can't imagine your being anything I wouldn't love. I love you, love you. I'll love you till I die."

She closed her eyes, overcome with the sweetness and pain of his words. Oh, dear, would he throw his arms about her there in the garden, pumpkin and all? But she wanted him to. She longed for him just to touch her hand.

"I've told Mother," she spoke falteringly. "She is in deep grief over me. She says the wrong is mine, not thine, and it is—it is. They would read me out of Meeting. Oh, Tom, why did thee come here?"

"Lydia, they need not despise me, these Quakers. I am a good man, Lydia. At least, I'm not wicked."

"Oh, Tom, haven't I known that from beginning?"

"Most people don't think so," he acknowledged. For Tom's gayety sat not well in the pious community.

"But I *know*," she answered.

Great heaven, the faith of her. Great heaven, the trust of her in him. He'd be good now, if he never saw her again.

"Do you want to break my heart?" he asked.

She could not answer this.

"Do you love me, Lydia?"

Her head bowed and he saw her shoulders quiver, though there was no sobbing.

"You said so once. Won't you say it again?"

"Yes, Tom. Oh, yes—yes. But I would be wicked to love anyone better than God and the true worship of God. And, oh, oh, I must not, I cannot be read out of Meeting."

"You would be disgraced, of course."

"Yes," she breathed.

"Are you quite sure it is not the disgrace that's holding you back? You know that God can be truly worshipped anywhere and by any true soul. Didn't your George Fox say something like that? Couldn't you love God and me too, Lydia?"

Tom had thought out all these arguments. Had he not lain awake nights thinking them? It was all so clear to him. But well he knew the stone wall of Quakerism against which he beat. That stone wall was here now.

He was astonished at the horror with which she looked up. The pumpkin slid from her arms down to the path. Then she hid her face in her two hands.

What had he done? Had he offended her so deeply as that?

But Tom asked none of these questions. They faded

before he could speak them—faded because, somehow, he knew she was suddenly separated from him, by a great gulf—a trance of the spirit. In his far voyages he had not been farther away from her than at this moment. It was all over with him. She would never marry him, now.

Would she never speak to him? Must he go away?

But now quietly Lydia lifted her head.

"Thee has shown me my error," she said in a small clear voice. "And the Lord has shown it me too. It was pride, not faith, that held me from thee. I shall marry thee, Tom Coffyn, whatever comes."

The unexpectedness of it! The dizziness of it! Tom seemed to be hurled upward like an arrow from black depth into bewildering light.

"Lydia—you don't mean—" He stumbled at it like an astonished boy. "Lydia, you darling saint!"

"Tom, oh, thee mustn't," she protested. "They'll see thee from the windows."

"Tell them it's your future husband kissing you," he answered rapturously.

Tom came to his senses and picked up the pumpkin.

"Shall we go in and tell them?" he asked.

"Yes," she answered steadily. But somehow the very joy in her eyes showed him the depth of her renunciation— the stark courage with which she meant to face her kith and kin.

"You sha'n't marry me out of Meeting, Lydia," he told her.

"Yes, I shall. I have decided."

"Bless your dear plucky heart. But you're not going to marry me out of Meeting, I tell you, I'm a Quaker now. From this moment I'm a Friend."

"Tom Coffyn." She drew away from him. "How dares thee jest at sacred things?"

"I'm not joking. I'm serious. I'm going to join the Quakers."

"But thee cannot become a Friend that way, just—just for love."

"Why not?" he demanded.

"Tom, Tom!" she cried in real distress. "Thee cannot do it to gain an end."

"But, Lydia, I'd gained the end beforehand. Look here, are you trying to drive me away from your faith?"

Something in his voice touched her with his real meaning. Tom had seen her religion in action. What did it mean, that deep withdrawal into the Unseen and the return with certain knowledge? A knowledge so wise, so happy for himself? It was real—that thing. It awed him.

And only think, last night he had made up his mind to test Lydia's love. Let her give up her Quakerism, if she loved him. If not—well, Tom had been angry. How crude that all seemed now.

"Yes, I'm a Friend," he said quietly. "We'll be married in Meeting, Lydia."

9. *The Perpetual Frontier*

TOM COFFYN'S CHANGE of religion was a nine-day wonder in Nantucket. Old Elias Coffyn said, he'd rather have *buried* Thomas. He stormed and threatened to disown him. But the tie between father and son had been one of severity, chiefly, and Tom remained loyal to his new faith.

Poor Tom. He little knew the kind of drubbing he'd get at the hands of his Quaker hosts. He reported himself to the Meeting. Then a committee waited upon him and questioned his private life till he blushed scarlet.

"Look here," he said. "I'm a decent fellow. I live decent whether I'm in the South Seas or in Nantucket. That's more than you can say of some of your own!"

But was this youth "convinced" or was he merely in love? That was a fine question to bother the old gray heads. Tom had to bring the most delicate motions of his spirit out to the light of day.

"I'll be hanged if I know which I loved first, God or Lydia," said Tom despairingly. "They're both mixed up together."

This answer almost cost him his membership. However they accepted him and passed their acceptances on to the Monthly Meeting where again it was duly deliberated. Then came the request for the marriage. More committees, more questions—the women waiting upon Lydia, the men upon Tom. Tom actually trembled lest some objection might even yet bar the way.

"But you'll marry me anyway, Lydia—won't you?" he assured himself.

"Yes, but thee must say 'thee'—not 'you,'" she warned him.

At last the great moment. Tom and Lydia, so freshly young—so conspicuously young—sat among the old dignitaries on the high seat facing the meeting.

First came the long silence. Then Tom, at his own discretion, rose, took Lydia's hand, and said the solemn words:

"I, Thomas, take thee, Lydia," and Lydia's clear voice answered the same words. There was no priest or minister.

"They must stand up bravely and marry themselves"—such was the sturdy Quaker saying. "It is a matter which does not concern an intermediate person but rests between the young folk and God."

Their certificate was signed by all the hundred and fifty guests.

(After all, was it so unwise, this solemn caring for the marriage of their young?)

Then, only a week later, Tom shipped in the new brig, *Touch-Me-Not*. He was twenty-two and captain. But youths were forward in those days.

Lydia, standing alone on the housetop within the white-fenced Walk, wondered how Martha White had "stood it" when her man went away to sea. The sails of the *Touch-Me-Not* lessened and grew less, fluttered to mere threads as the ship changed her course off Great Point—so defenseless a speck in the gray expanse—so infinitely precious—her dear one held within that tiny thing.

Suddenly Lydia turned with bowed head and disappeared down the dark hatch.

"Ain't she cold-hearted, though," quoth Liza Anne Renuff, who, from her housetop, was watching too. "Goin' downstairs when her husband's ship's still in plain sight."

Liza Anne could not see the young wife locked in her lonely bedroom, nor the agony of stifled sobs which swept her there. Lydia stayed locked in her bedroom for three hours. After which time she came out to her spinning wheel and spun steadily all day without stopping for meals.

This day began for Lydia that habit of solitary prayer which grew upon her as the years went by—hours alone locked in her room.

"Lydia Coffyn's not resigned to her husband's going away like most women," said a sharp-sighted member of her meeting. "She pretends to be, but she isn't. There's a look to her. I know. If she had a shop now in Petticoat Lane to keep her busy, it would be better for her."

Dionis was born. But even the coming of so gay a little maiden—"the image of her father"—did not cure Lydia. For she was walled about with an implacable reserve. Tom Coffyn, and he only, had broken down that wall and brought to her the light and life which so amazed her. Now he was gone, and with his going went the light. She could only wait like one in prison for his return. This loneliness bred in Lydia a severity.

"Dionis, wipe thy feet at the door. I have just swept the room." This was the welcome for Dencey when she returned from school.

"Mother, I saw the cunningest little bird on the shore. He ran right in the big, big combers and wasn't afraid."

"What was thee doing on the shore, Dionis? Thee should come straight home."

So the wall was built between Lydia and her little girl.

All Dencey's childhood was chaptered and divisioned by her father's returns—those glorious returns so longed for in the household, prayed for every morning in family prayer.

The first of these she did not really remember, standing, a round-eyed child of three, in the doorway behind her mother. But all Nantucket remembered it, so it was just as if she did. Tom dashed up the pretty, decorous steps and threw both arms about his Quaker wife standing at the top, kissing her rapturously three times. All the street saw him, but Liza Anne Renuff saw him best, for she had a side window for "seeing the pass."

"Lyddy was like to die," declared Liza Anne. "And I should think she would, him kissin' her before the whole of Fair Street. 'Come into the house, Thomas,' she says. 'And that I will,' he answers, and she fair pulls him in an' shuts the door. Then he says—"

"How does thee know what he said with the door shut, Liza Anne?" asked her listener.

"Oh, that Peggy from Tom Never's Head that Lyddy adopted—she was on the stairs. She told me the hull of it and—"

Liza Anne always took breath in the middle of a sentence, so it was a fine art to interrupt her.

"And *he* says, just as if they weren't married, 'My love,

my love, I've longed so to see thee. Just thee—no one else'; and she stops him—'Thomas, thee forgets the child.' With that, he turned around and saw Dencey lookin' up with those round eyes of hers.

" 'Lydia, not our baby, this great girl!' he cries out. Why is it the men folks is so astonished that childer grow up while they're gone? But then, o'course, he'd never clapped eyes on Dencey before, that's some excuse. Anyway, Peg says all his wild ways stopped to once, an' he picked up Dencey in his arms, an' looked at her face as if she'd been a ghost or somethin'—and *then*, what does thee think he said?—

" 'Thou dear little Impossible!'

"Now, what kind o' a name was that to call his own Christian child? Well, anyways, Dencey seemed to like it. She just cuddled down against his neck quick.

" 'Thomas, she knows thee for her father!' says Lyddy.

"With that, Dencey laughed the cutest little laugh, all half smothered against her father's coat. 'Why, she never laughed like that before,' says Lyddy.

"Well, I could 'a' told her why—Lyddy never petted the child that way. Not she."

After this began a happy time for the little girl—a time not defined in her memory, but which entered into the texture of her days. There were long walks in the sunshine holding Father's hand. They were standing on the shore, and the tiny teetersnipes with their legs like flowerstems were running on the sand in the white thin carpet of foam. Such funny, smart little birds. And the great breakers roared and smashed down, but never touched them. And Father said, "Dionis, I hope someday thee'll have faith like those little birds."

And Dencey wondered what he meant.

Then it was winter. Father coming into the house shaking off the snow like a great bear and laughing, laughing. And Mother ran to him—as if she had been frightened—and threw both arms about him and said, "Thank God," twice. Then there was a day when Hopestill came and Dencey had a party for her doll with codfish vertebræ for cups and scallop shells for plates.

Oh, a happy magic time!

And, meanwhile, the grown-ups were in a bitterness which they knew not how to bear.

The War of 1812 was a calamity which might well make them quail. For Nantucket was and is a perpetual frontier. No government can afford protection to this outpost of the sea, and no government did so. The Revolutionary sufferings were not yet forgotten by Nantucketers, and now, in 1812, the people left the Island by families and clans. Sixty houses were left vacant in the little town. Those who stuck to their Island knew not what each day would bring forth. The waters about them were full of the enemy's ships. Their whaling fleet, one hundred and fifty strong, dwindled to nothing—the ships huddling into Nantucket Harbor for protection.

Lydia thanked God every night in special prayer that her man was not on the high seas to be captured by the British and left to rot in the hold of a prison ship—that most dreaded of all.

But, in spite of being at home, Tom was in constant danger. He took charge of a packet which ran the blockade to New York to get wood and flour for the Nantucketers. Fuel there was none, and the winter the coldest ever known. Foodstuffs grew scarce. Hungry people begged in the streets, an unchancy sight for a self-respecting New England town.

Time and again, Tom Coffyn's packet was chased by the enemy, fired upon, and got away only by his superior seamanship.

By the fireside in the evening, Dencey would hear him telling stories. They always seemed to end, "And by and by the Britisher was hull-under and this morning not a stick of her to be seen." Father could tell stories as no one else could tell them.

But Dencey's clearest recollection was of the day when Peace was declared. How the bells rang! How even Mother ran down town to make sure the news was true, and how Dencey clung to her hand and wondered at the people running hither and thither in State Street and some really grown-up people crying aloud.

She saw old Captain Parker on a little sled, a child's sled but hitched to a horse. American flags were flying from both horse and sled. Frost sparkled on his bushy eyebrows and on his muffler where his breath touched. He was starting out to the Commons, and everybody cheered.

"I'm goin' to get to Polpis and Quidnet, if I can," he said.

"Oh, Mother, I wish I could go on the cunning little sleigh," said Dencey. "It'll be such a nice ride."

"Indeed it will not, child, Captain Parker will be fortunate if he doesn't get stalled in the snow."

"Then, why does he go?"

"To carry the news. So the people on the lonely farms can stop their fear. Oh, how wonderful that we need not be listening now every night for pirates and invaders."

10. *The Family on Fair Street*

BUT NOW, WITH the coming of Peace, Father, of course, went to sea again.

This came out of the blue, as all calamity does in childhood. There had been Father with them—established—one of the unalterables of life. Then, suddenly, Dionis was crouching by the newel post in the front hall. She sat grasping the spindles of the stair rail in voiceless fear, hid under Father's great sea cloak, which he had thrown over the post.

Father and Mother were in the parlor, beyond the shut door, saying good-bye. But they didn't say it! Dionis listened miserably to the death-like silence. At last came Father's voice, like a deep viol—just a sentence—and Mother's low answer—a single word. Then the terrible tragic silence again.

All of a sudden, after an eternity, the parlor door flung open. They came out, and Father, in a great hurry, snatched up his cloak.

"Why, Dionis Coffyn!" exclaimed Lydia. "Go back to the kitchen at once." Her voice had a sharp edge from the stress within.

But Dencey sprang up to her father.

"Father! Don't go!" She wailed.

Father held her close and tried to quiet her sobbing. She felt his cheek wet against her own. But Mother was not crying. "Mother," she decided, "did not care." It was one of those swift child-judgments from which there is no appeal, and of which the grown-up is so unconscious.

Then there was Father running fast down the doorsteps, struggling into his coat as he went—the awful finality of his back and bowed head.

Dionis ran out to the kitchen and climbed sobbing into Peggy's lap.

"Oh, Peggy," she said. "The ocean goes so far—right into the sky."

Peggy patted her shoulder.

"There, there!" she crooned. "Cryin' when thee's so fortunate. Two years thy father's been home. Thee'll be lucky if he stays two months next time. Some of 'em is off again in a fortnit."

During the following months and years, Dionis was conscious of a suspense that hung about the house and all its doings. The suspense was in Lydia's mind really, but Dencey caught it somehow—reflecting like a small mirror. Perhaps the daily mention of that far sea-journeying, perhaps those instinctive haltings of Lydia in front of Tom Coffyn's portrait—the sigh as she turned to work. However the suspense came, it was as if all things in the household waited an event. All things were held back for Tom Coffyn's return.

Of course, there were home happenings. Lydia's brother Stephen's wife died while Stephen was at sea. The wife died giving birth to her twelfth child. Nine children were living, and all these, including the hour-old baby, Lydia took into her household. Thus Dionis acquired overnight a great flock of brothers and sisters. There was Jane the oldest, such a help to Mother, Steve, Bob, Jared, and Elkanah the four boys, who teased Dionis with terrific but wholesome discipline. There was Rosie the cripple, Dencey's age. Then the little boys Homer and Barna, and lastly the tiny baby Hannah.

Lydia did not hesitate one single hour in assuming this burden. There was always a downrightness about Lydia's good deeds.

"Just think," she said, "when Steve comes back, he'll feel he still has a home and the children all together."

Of course, Peggy Runnel was always there in the house. Another of Lydia's pensioners.

Peggy's father and mother lived in a cottage far out on the Commons near Tom Never's Head. It was one of those tiny gray cots that can be glimpsed beyond the fluid rolling of the moors like loneliness made visible. One night, during the War of 1812, they heard footsteps around that desert place and pistol shots. Then the door burst open and Britishers from an invading vessel were all over the house. They took the hams from the chimney, the bread from the oven, all their little store of flour and cornmeal. It was in vain that Mrs. Runnel told them her children would starve. "There's no more food on the Island and no way to get any," she told them. But spite of this, they took all, and carried Mr. Runnel away as prisoner.

Kind folk in Nantucket town gave of their scanty stores to help the stricken ones, and Lydia took Peggy—just ten years old—promising to keep her till the father returned.

But Peggy always cried so bitterly at the mention of going back home that finally the matter was abandoned and Peggy became one of the family.

Wonderful times were those in the great basement kitchen of the Fair Street house, wonderful for a little girl to experience, and, in remembrance, a fragrance for the whole of her life. Big as a town hall, that kitchen was, with a broad fireplace to match. Always crowded, full of the vivid life that youngsters bring, as one brings into the warmth the invigorating air of a winter night.

Grandmother sat in her corner knitting, Lydia in the firelight whirled her spinning wheel, Jane carded wool or helped Dionis to sew her sampler. The older boys hulled walnuts sitting on the floor on an old spread-out sail. The walnuts came from the Cape, for there was only one walnut tree on the Island. Steve had traded them off a ship.

"Come on, Dence, help hull 'em. They won't make thy hands any browner than what they are." So Steve taunted her.

Dionis ran to her mother, holding out both little fists. "*Are* they brown, Mother?" she demanded. "Are they darker than Steve's?"

And Lydia, looking, said softly:

"Child, they are the image of thy father's hands."

Sometimes Lydia read from *Fox's Journal* and Dionis would doze off over her sampler. Again Lydia would put aside the book and tell the adventures of the saints of Quakerdom, saying:

"I read this to-day, in *Besse's Sufferings.*"

Then Dionis would lean forward, elbows on knees, and eyes wide and eager. For *Besse's Sufferings* was a book of life and adventures that know no fear.

And, oh, the "company" they had! Young men, cousins all, just landed from the sea. Jane was pretty, and they came to chat with her. They were hardly older than Steve, but they had had their four years on the other side of the world. They told of forbidden coasts—a country called Japan where no man might land. It had a pure white cone-shaped mountain that seemed to hover in the sky, not touching earth at all.

They told of desolate islands where there were no women—none whatever.

"Gracious," one would say with a glance at Jane, "I'm glad I don't live there." And the appreciative titter went round.

They told of trees that bore bread, of savage men who would eat Nantucketers, of flowers that poured out such pollen as to streak the hands with honey, of auroras in the Antarctic, of sandalwood isles whose perfume wafted leagues over the sea.

And they told of whales.

Gideon Whippy—a big, black-haired lad—was a harpooner. He it was who must stand at the prow of the little whale boat holding ready his spear-like harpoon until they were in veritable touching distance of the vast whale's side.

"Yes," he said, nodding his young head proudly, "I gave her her medicine, for sure. I stabbed the critter right back of her fin—to the vitals, first lick. My, but she spouted blood high as the masthead, an' she beat her fins so it sounded like cannon shots. Then she swum off. We just coasted after her, an' the line ran out so fast that the gunwale smoked fire. Then she sounded. Jiminy, but we had to act quick or we would 'a' been with Davy Jones's locker."

Great boasting this, but nobody blamed him—least of

all Jane.

These young folk had no dancing, no music, nor cards to play. They took their pleasure in talk, and they were famous talkers. And Lydia always brought out puddings and pound-rounds for such young cousins just off the sea. They'd had hardtack so long.

To the Coffyn fireside came also the long succession of Quaker preachers "under concern" to visit Nantucket—remarkable men and women from New England, Philadelphia, North Carolina, Old England, and France. Some of them were solemn and forbidding to the little girl. But to most of them religion meant adventure. They had pushed into the heart of the American wilderness in their ardor for Christ.

William Williams came from the Whitewater Meeting in Indiana. He was a notable preacher. But people might come fifty miles to hear him and sit in silence through the whole meeting. He spoke only if the Spirit moved him. "Does thee suppose," he said to one who complained of this, "that I would journey so far, leaving my dear wife and the comforts of home, on a message of my own?"

At the South Meeting House in Nantucket he preached three hours, "yet at the end the people did not rise to go, their minds being under a covering so solemn." This was for the grown-ups. Dencey remembered only how tender and merry was his glance, resting upon her, and how she sat all evening, her little hand in his, while he talked to the others by the keeping-room fire.

But, best of all, to Dencey's mind was the coming of old Selah Wetherstone. Selah sat by the kitchen hearth, brown and wrinkle-faced, with eyebrows bushy and so long that Barna pulled them once with his fingers.

Selah had been with Father through the whole *Touch-Me-Not* voyage. But homeward bound he had fallen from the masthead and broken both his legs.

"That thar put me in dry-dock," Selah would say ruefully. "Don't spose I'll ever git off the ways agin. I seem to be mended, but I don't answer the wheel."

Selah could make ships. Oh, such little, little ships! He would whittle them with his knife and fit on tiny silken sails and impossibly small rails and anchors. The masts, sails, and all would lie flat on the deck. At last would come the great moment. Selah would put the ship into a bottle and quickly jerk a string, when, presto, all the masts and sails would fly upright.

"Now," he'd assert triumphantly. "Won't the landlubber be a-sayin', 'How'd ye ever git that thar ship int' the bottle!' "

Selah talked unendingly of his "vyges." "Ben round the Horn three times. Nasty place with its fogs an' high cliffs, an' the winds pouncin' off of 'em like cats. Glory, the porpoises we ketched thar! We had porpoise-liver patties fur two days. Better nor any calves' liver ye ever tasted. Captain Coffyn he was allus fur givin' his men good feedin'. Not like some that 'ud like it ef the men could live on corn husks the hull endurin' vyge. Onct we went into Callao, and Cap'n Coffyn, he got a lot of green vegetables an' these here mangoes an' melons an' fresh meat. An' he give 'em to us same as the cabin. But the men they don't much like sich eatin'. 'Twa'n't three days afore they was complainin' and growlin', callin' for their salt horse. Salt horse's best fur vyges, anyways. Give me salt horse every time, what ye kin eat before goin' to bed an' feel it all night long a-lyin' on yer stummick and a-nourishin' of ye."

It might be observed that, whenever Selah came in, Lydia put aside her buzzing wheel and took some voice-less task, or sometimes even sat in the corner with her hands in her lap—unheard-of idleness. For sooner or later Selah always came 'round to his Cap'n Coffyn.

"Sailed with many a cap'n in my life, but never a better nor Tom Coffyn—but never a *queerer* too—I'll say that. Never a queerer! Why, looky hyar, when we struck that school o' whales off the Fijis an' killed an' cut in as fast as we could pound, Cap'n Coffyn he just goes 'round the deck as if it was pilot bread fur breakfast. But when we diskivered a island, why he was excited as a grasshopper. He takes latitiude an' longitude, he axes every man jack has he ever known of a island in this here location. Then nothin' would do but we must make a landin'. Though, crickit! we was glad enough after rollin' around in that tub out o' sight o' land fur three months. Well, we goes int' the lagoon—a pretty little place—with beaches an' palm trees. An' the fust thing Cap'n Coffyn jumps out on the sand he says, 'I name this here island Lydia Island.' Then he goes up int' the woods. Dangerous, that is. Ye can't tell what kind o' pizen ye'll run acrost—flower or critter or man. But it's flowers the Cap'n is after. Much more pleased with them than whales. He's like a boy in an apple orchard. He's got a log book an' writes an' writes. I see it afterward in the cabin when I was swabbin' up the floor—pictures of every one o' them flowers and long hea-then names to 'um. An' 'explanations,' he calls 'em, but when ye gits through readin' of 'em, ye don't know near's much about that thar flower as ye did afore. Hit was more like talkin' about firearms—all pistils an' stamins an' sich."

"Well, Mis' Coffyn," said Selah suddenly. "Not long afore yer good man gits home, eh?"

Lydia started as if from a dream. "Yes," she answered. "Almost four years. I do expect him now almost any day."

How astonished was Dencey.

A lifetime had passed since Father had gone away. Then she was a tiny child in a shadowy world—now a big girl who could go to school and know with clear conscious-ness what went on about her.

"Oh, Mother, will he truly truly come?" she cried, jump-ing up and clapping her hands.

Then Selah went home, but not until Lydia had filled his pocket with thick ginger cookies. It occurred to Dionis that Mother liked Selah to come. This was very strange, for even Dionis could see that he was not a gentleman. He smelt so fishy—just like the docks—and Peggy said he only took a bath on Independence Day.

"Yes," said Mother softly, as she opened the door. "Next time thee comes, Selah, maybe Captain Coffyn will be here to greet thee."

11. *A Wonderful Night*

IT WAS ONLY a week later that Lydia received a letter from her husband brought by the hand of Captain Joy home from his voyage. The letter was four months old, but that was not bad for South Pacific mail.

My Amiable Wife [it ran]:

We have just fallen in with the ship *Five Brothers* and had a gam this morning. They are homeward bound, so I have the prized opportunity of communicating with my beloved wife.

I am sorry to say this voyage has been far less successful than my former ones as captain. These whaling grounds where we now are (Lat. 15 south, Long. 110 west) seem about killed out, and spite of our best efforts, the ship's hold is only half filled. Captain Joy advises our seeking the newly discovered grounds in the Japan Sea, and after much deliberation I have determined to go there. I cannot tell thee, my beloved Lydia, the pain this decision has cost me. I had hoped within a few months to be with thee and my darling daughter. Now that joy will be deferred another year. It is very difficult for me to bow to this ruling of Providence. My only comfort is that, with thy greater faith and flowering of the Seed, thee will be able to accept it with resignation and serenity.

There is no news here. Last month we landed upon an island where I discovered a species of lily which I believe has never been classified or described. If such proves to be the case, I shall name it Lilium Lydiense. May I say that in its fresh beauty upon its stalk it reminded me of thee.

Thy ever loving husband,
Thomas Coffyn.

Lydia read the letter in her locked bedroom. Then called Dionis and told her its contents. Dionis did not cry. Father's coming had grown to be a mythical thing, anyway. But it gave her a feeling of desolation that was the worse because so strange to her. Perhaps this too was reflected from Lydia's white face.

"Will he ever come?" Dionis asked.

"Yes," Lydia answered. "I know that he will."

If, within the next few weeks, anyone had noticed Lydia (which nobody did), he might have seen an added severity with the children, sharp judgments of her neighbors, even a frequent burning of her fingers at the cooking. After that came a tranquillity of face and gesture; and Lydia, who spoke seldom, spoke still less. The Divine Seed had flowered into Resignation.

So two months passed.

One night Dionis, who was sleeping with her mother in the front room upstairs, was wakened by a sound at the window. It came again, just as if someone had thrown a pebble.

"Why, they'll break the pane," thought Dionis. Her mother slept on. Baby Hannah had been ill and Lydia had lost much sleep.

"Mother," cried Dencey. "Somebody's throwin' pebbles on the window."

Lydia roused slowly. "Oh, no, child, thee's been dreaming. Go to sleep—"

"*Crack*" went the sound again. And Lydia sprang from the bed and opened the window.

It was moonlight, but the intruder was in shadow.

"Who wants me?" inquired Lydia. "Is anybody sick?"

"I want thee!" came up the answer. "And I am abundantly well."

The joyous voice brought a rush of memory.

"Mother, it's Father!" squeaked Dencey, in amaze.

But Lydia was already throwing her big shawl about her. She sped down the stairway like a swallow—fumbled at the lock, flung open the front door. Father caught her in his arms.

"Lydia, my darling!"

Then Dencey too was enveloped in the woolly fresh-aired embrace. He dragged her to the moonlit door.

"I must see thy face. Oh, such a big grown-up daughter. Just thyself. Not like anybody at all."

"I didn't expect thee," Mother was saying, "thy letter—"

"Yes—yes, and right after it came a school of whales. We couldn't kill and cut in fast enough. Oh, Lydia, God is good. I am home—home!"

They crowded with nervous laughter through the hallway to the keeping room. Here Mother started to rake open the fire. But Father brushed her aside.

"What has thee a big husband for if he can't mend fire for thee?" he said. And he raked the red embers clear, piled on thin kindling and wood in quantities never allowed in the house. In an instant the room blossomed into rosy light.

Then he hugged Mother over again.

"I must go upstairs and get dressed," she said.

"No, no, thee looks so pretty wrapped like an Indian. And how long thy hair is, Lydia. Let's stay here a moment. Just us three. Here, Dencey daughter, thee'll take cold."

And he snatched off his greatcoat and wrapped the nightgowned Dencey as if she had been a baby. Then set her up bundle-wise in a chair.

"Look there," he said, with a glance at the front window, "the Smiths all lighted up too. Joe came up home when I did."

Joe Smith was his second mate, and his home was across the street.

Now, with a clatter-bang, Steve and Bob and Elkanah came like an avalanche downstairs.

"Uncle Tom's home!" they shouted.

And Father could not imagine where all the boys had come from until Mother hurriedly explained. She had written when she took Steve's children in, but Father had not got the letter.

Then Mother and Dionis went upstairs quickly and dressed and hurried down to get breakfast.

What delightful strangeness to have breakfast in the middle of the night. For it was only four o'clock even yet.

"Oh, to drink thy coffee again, Lydia," cried Father,

following her about and bothering everything in the kitchen. "Thy coffee and thy popovers."

"That's a hint," retorted Lydia, in a voice that seemed all pent-up laughter—not like Mother's voice at all.

After breakfast, the dawn came strange too, like rose-colored magic—then full day, and a cart clattered up to the house with Father's sea chest.

12. *Out of the Orient*

FATHER WAS LIKE a boy opening the great sea chest. They all crowded around. First he took out a *swift*, pure white, of whale ivory—delicate spokes whereon she could wind her wool.

"I made it for thee," he said. "It whiled away many an hour waiting for whales."

Then came a whale-ivory button for the newel post in the front hall. Then the pink cameo shell which Dionis was to treasure so many years.

"It was a real flower," he explained. "I copied it carefully. The little dove in the center is far plainer than I could draw it."

He was on his favorite theme, and must needs tell the genus and species of the flower, its habit of growth, its scent.

Until Bob ventured:

"Say, Uncle Tom. There's lots more in the chest."

"Oh, you boys—I'd have had presents for every one of you if I'd known you were here. But I'll find something for you aboard the *Touch-Me-Not*, never fear."

Then he dived again and brought forth a little box.

"Hold thy apron, Dencey," he said.

Dionis held out her full skirt, and into it Father poured a rainbow tide of shimmering, slithering shells.

"I gathered these for thee on little lonely islands where foot of man had never trod."

Dionis gasped. The color caught her with a sharp pleasure almost like pain. Without a word she gathered up her treasures, spread them upon a table and began busily sorting the colors. There were purple shells, shells of delicate lavender, shells like a tiny sunrise of rose, shells milkwhite. She crooned to them as she touched them.

"Dionis," said Mother's voice, "isn't thee going to thank Father?"

Dionis had been shy of the tall impulsive stranger with those smile lines about his mouth, etched by the winds of two hemispheres. But now she turned with outspread arms, ran to him, and hugged him close about the neck.

Then she returned to her crooning task, she knew not how long.

She was roused by a sweet unearthly scent—a scent full of the mystery of the Orient—that Orient of the old days which was all romance, with no menace.

She looked up. The decorous familiar room was rollicking in beauteous confusion. A white-embroidered shawl hung with flexile drenched folds over the chest lid, Quaker gray silk, yards and yards of it, billowed over a chair—gray but shot through with lavender like a hidden melody.

"I got these from China," Father was explaining.

But upon another chair was that which held Dencey's attention. Two Chinese rose jars—one of intense azure—

a color that seemed to think. Another of translucent white glaze with figures upon it, a woman and her children about her, all with pink, dreamy faces, living and real. A beauty seemed to bloom from the vases and pervade the very air. They drew Dencey to them. She fell upon her knees in front of the chair, looking close, clasping her hands because she knew she must not touch them.

Suddenly came Lydia's voice.

"Dionis Coffyn, whatever is thee doing, kneeling that way? Thee looks as if thee was praying to those heathen vases."

Dionis started, scrambled to her feet. A wave of tears swept her and she ran from the room.

Up in the attic she crouched behind a little hair trunk sobbing. What was this misery like a bat's wing that hurt her so abominably? She was bitterly ashamed that anyone should have seen her kneeling to the vases—terribly angry at Mother, who had made the others look at her. And she was afraid—she did not know of what. She sobbed a long while.

Suddenly there was a leaping step upon the stairs, and Father's voice calling:

"Daughter, where is thee?"

Dionis kept hidden, but Father found her and drew her out from behind the trunk. Oh, now, if he asked questions, she would be undone!

"Did thee know," he asked casually, "that thee left all thy pretty shells on the table? I gathered them into the box for thee. And here is the blue vase. I brought it for Mother. But she says thee can have it because she has the other one."

His arm was about her. Where was the strange trouble

now? The bat's wing of it had flown out of the window—
and all the childish anger against Mother.

"Father," said Dionis busily, "I'm going to make flowers out of my shells. Jane makes ugly ones, but I'll make
pretty ones. Thee'll see."

13. *Father and Dencey*

T HIS TIME FATHER stayed at home only eight weeks. But these were long enough for the growth of a tree of life—the understanding between Dionis and her father. It sent roots deep into the heart of the little girl, and its foliage spread through all her growing thought.

Father took her for long walks in the Commons.

"Why, Tom," Lydia said, "the berries aren't ripe yet."

"Is it sheep-shearin' time?" inquired little Barna.

"No," laughed Tom Coffyn. "I guess we're going because the sky is there."

Father showed her the flowers, explained them as though she were grown up, and taught her the long Latin names. He even took her to one of the lonely beaches to swim—an unheard-of performance. Dionis romped like a boy in the tingling water. But as she wore a long calico dress and underclothes, and the dress was modestly weighted with shot, the swimming was not a success.

"An' how should it be," quoth Peggy when they came home. "Who ever heard of a girl swimmin'? I'd think thee'd be ashamed, Dencey Coffyn."

"I didn't have time to be ashamed," laughed Dionis. "The ocean knocked me down quicker'n I could get up, and when I laughed, it knocked me down more. It was like a big funny person."

Then Father went away again and became part of the long ago.

And then came the great change.

Father might journey around the Horn, but the difference to him was not so great as was this change to the little girl—the removal from Fair to North Water Street—oh, another planet! Infancy was definitely left behind in the old home. Girlhood began in the North Water Street house. It was Grandfather Coffyn's house, and Mother had moved there to take care of Grandfather, who was suddenly disabled and could go to sea no more. Grandfather had the great front room to himself, the room where Great-grandmother's picture hung and the flower piece of wax flowers under glass stood on the table. It was here that he called Dencey in, each First Day, and persistently taught her Congregationalist doctrine about hell and her soul. Mother said it was not true doctrine, but it haunted Dencey and made her afraid.

Mother had her own room. And Dionis (oh, wonderful, this!) was given a room all to herself on the third floor at the back, whose windows beheld the sea. As for the others, Steve, Jane, and the rest, they spread hither and yon over the whole vast house.

In Mother's room was born the beloved new baby, not a cousin, but Mother's own son and Dionis's brother. They called him Ariel, for that was the name of a Coffyn Grandfather 'way back in the sixteen hundreds. Dionis could not but love him more than Hannah and Barna and Kanah, for he was her very own.

Hopestill, who lived next door now, became Dencey's inseparable companion. Together they walked each morning to the Coffin School, a long walk clear across Nantucket town.

So Dionis came to the time when she threw the fateful stone at Jetsam. And so had to teach him to read "to make up."

BOOK THREE

14. *Meeting Jetsam*

WHY IS IT the children of the very poor always wear garments four sizes too big for them? Sammie Jetsam's pea-jacket would have fitted a grown sailorman, and hence it flopped dejectedly about his ankles. Perhaps this was just as well, for the rain fell in torrents.

Sammie Jetsam trudged along in the open Common where no path was. His little figure possessed the landscape solely. There was not even a house in sight, only the dreary Common, gray in the rain. Sammie walked slowly, swearing softly to himself. His thin little face under the great hat was as bleak as the weather. Sometimes, as solitary children do, he spoke aloud.

"She wun't come," he emphasized with his heel. "Not her!"

And a little later:

"Gals like her made o' silk and sugar what melts in the rain. She wun't come."

But he trudged onward, nevertheless.

Now, up over the misty horizon, loomed the stunted pine where Dencey Coffyn was to meet him. He didn't even look at it. He was quite close when he saw something fluttering by the tree.

"Whillikins!" he exclaimed. "Gee Whillikins!"

He began to run.

It was indeed Dencey Coffyn.

She stood under the tree, grasping with all her strength a big convulsing umbrella that threatened every moment to lift her bodily from the earth. It was quite useless as an umbrella. The rain swept under it so that her dress was soaked and her face glistened with wet. She was so occupied in her contest with the wind that she did not see Jetsam until he spoke to her.

"Daggon't, I didn't think ye'd come."

Dencey's eyes opened in amazement.

"Didn't I say I'd come?" she demanded.

"Yes, ye did, but hit's rainin'."

"Is that the reason thee's late? Thee mustn't be late," she added nervously. "I haven't got time. And thee didn't bring the book."

"Yes, I did, though," and Jetsam drew from the folds of the pea-jacket the precious *Pilgrim's Progress.*

"Open it," she commanded.

Dencey began forthwith.

"The first word there is *now—N,* say it!"

Jetsam sullenly complied.

"*O*—does thee remember the *o* I told thee."

Jetsam nodded.

"*W.*"

"Crimps, that's a long name for sich a small letter," he said.

"*W*'s a very proud letter," commented the teacher. "And the next word's *Vanity.*"

Never was teaching under greater difficulty. The two shivery figures crouched close together, and the two red little noses sniffled in concert. Now the wind seized the page and beat a thrilling tattoo with the corner of it.

"There's no use to swear at the wind," declared Dencey. "It won't stop. Besides, swearing's futile. Mother said so. Now put thy finger on *V* so as to keep the place."

The grubby finger touched the letter. Instantly the loosened page tore across in the wind.

Jetsam stamped his foot.

"I can't do it nohow," he stormed. "This hyar rain'll spile the book. I'm goin' home." He banged the book to.

Immediately an enormous relief came to Dencey. If Jetsam didn't want to learn, she was free. She could go back home and tell Mother. Mother would forgive or punish her, it mattered little which, for Dencey would be home again, safe in the old ways she knew. She needn't come out here ever again.

She watched Jetsam almost with a smile. He was opening the book again to find the torn place—oh, very carefully, lest the wind catch it. His hand trembled and his head bent lower—lower.

Suddenly, the pathos of his unletteredness swept her all over again. It was there—the stern "I must" which had brought her out into wind and rain. She glared at him over her two grasping hands which held the umbrella.

"No, thee won't go home, Sam Jetsam," she rang out. "I had to run away to get here. And—and I told my mother a lie. And now thee's just got to learn something to pay up."

His head was still down.

"I won't larn from no gal," he said sullenly.

"Then, why'd thee make me teach thee?"

He stood still a puzzled moment.

"We could go to Brown's barn," he conceded. "It don't leak but a smidjin."

"Then we'll go there," she answered in a fateful voice.

Up the storm-blurred hillside toiled the two valiant little figures, Jetsam ahead, Indian fashion, and Dionis following with the careening umbrella. Surely Parnassus was never more steeply climbed.

They were fairly swept into the barn by the last obstreperous gust. Inside, the old building swayed and creaked. There were low roars, and high fine screechings of wind as if from witch instruments. But it was haven. The damp hay had a wine-like smell.

"The hay's in the loft," said Jetsam. "Let's go up. An' nobody'll see us thar, neither."

They climbed the ladder, found a soft nest, and once more opened the book.

But here Jetsam faced his real problem. With all impediments removed, he was assailed by that strange inertia which stands at the beginning of all mental effort. His mind, never brought into subjection, baulked like a bad horse. He was shy, resentful, ashamed, and immeasurably stupid. He had no defense except the small boy's—trying to be funny.

"*Pil*grim," he announced smartly. "Did he sell pills, then? War he a doctor?"

"Of course he wasn't. Is thee going to begin, Sam Jetsam?"

"Say, ye ought to see Jill when she's drunk. She staggers around like this."

Dionis regarded him with infinite scorn.

"Sam Jetsam," she said. "Thee's just mocking an' hectoring. If thee doesn't want to learn, I can go home this minute. And I'll not come again. I can tell thee that."

She jumped up from the hay, fluttered her skirts into order. He knew she meant what she said. He caught at her skirt with two frightened hands.

"Set down," he pleaded. "I'll git it somehow."

And "git it" he did—one letter after another—whole words even. Difficult ones like Vanity Fair, which he recognized no matter in what corner of the page they hid. He bent over the book in a hungry eagerness.

"Now I know seven whole words. Tell me another. What's this hyar one with the long tow o' letters trailin' after ut? Now, see if I kin say them fust ones."

Dencey bent to her task, flushed and eager—meeting his questions. Time passed. She was all unaware.

Suddenly she looked up.

"Oh. It's a long time. I must go. I'll be late to tea, and then—and Mother—!"

"Will yer ma whup ye?" questioned Jetsam, following her hastening form down the ladder.

"No, she doesn't believe in it."

"Then what yer 'fraid of?"

"I'm not afraid."

But she was. Jetsam could well see that this little aristocrat, so protected in a world he knew not, was bitterly afraid. It was his first sense of kinship with her.

"Who will whup ye if yer ma won't?" he asked.

"Grandfather might. But I'm not afraid of that."

No, it was not a corporeal fear. It was different, this. She was an outlander. She belonged to this rainy windy world out on the Commons, exposed to dangers and knowledges which she could not guess. Home could not enfold her. Responsibility—the heavy pressing sense of it was upon Dencey—setting her the long, long task. It was bred into her by her pioneer ancestry, her Quaker ancestry. She could no more resist responsibility than she could the color of her eyes and hair.

Now she was at the wide barn door. With many a struggle, she opened the umbrella. She stepped out.

With one huge burst the wind turned her umbrella wrong-side out. Dencey burst into tears.

"It's ruined," she exclaimed desperately. "Mother's umbrella. She'll ask me, an' I'll—I'll have to lie again."

Jetsam took it with almost a gentle gesture. It was one of those huge drab affairs well nigh as proper as the Meeting House itself. Slowly he bent it back, holding the ribs in place until the fluttering bony rag was its former useful self.

"Thar," he said proprietarily. "Don't ye put it up agin. Ye've got to reef everything in this hyar gale."

She tucked it under her arm and hurried forward, bending her bonneted head in the rain.

"Ye come back agin to-morrow," he shouted after her.

"No—Mother needs me. Next day I'll come—after school."

He hurried after her.

"I hain't forgive ye yit," he said. "Recollect that. Ye've got to come."

Then he stood in the road and watched her go—the terrible wind ballooning her skirts as she struggled down the path. Even yet he did not trust that she would come again!

15. *Brown's Barn*

DENCEY'S NEXT expedition to the Brown barn, so dreaded by her, proved to be as easy as the first had been difficult. Mother was away helping Martha White with her new store. So Dencey did not even have to make the excuse of going to Aunt Lovesta's.

It was real spring—the Commons a vivid green. Violets looked up at her from the path with friendly eyes. In the distances were purple carpets of them.

Jetsam waited for her at the top of the hill. They climbed together into the fragrant hay. The hay-door was open, looking out over the field spaces to the stark surprise of azure sea. How differently this spoke to each of them! To the girl, Father's ship sailing somewhere on the other side of the world; to the boy, a whaler outward bound and he, shipped as cabin boy. Of course, neither of them spoke this. The sea was as common as the straight mantelshelf above the fireplace, or the grass by the cabin door.

Dionis immediately took out of her school satchel a sheet of paper—two sheets torn from one of Grandfather's old logs.

"I made this for thee. It'll help," she said.

There stood the letters of the alphabet in straight columns like print and a picture to each letter. Jetsam gazed with bulging eyes.

"Ye never," he asserted. "Ye couldn't make that thar."

Jetsam never spoke a tentative statement. It was always flat, fight-provoking argument.

"I did too," said Dionis.

"Why, look at this hyar bird flyin' by the second letter. Hits like a book-pictur'."

"I made it," she asserted again. "I guess I wouldn't say so if I didn't. I don't tell l—"

She stopped as though a hand were laid upon her mouth. Could she, Dencey Coffyn, any longer say, "I don't tell lies"? Why, when she was making these very letters, Mother had asked her "What for," and she had replied, "For the children at school." Oh, a lie every day! And how could she ever stop it!

Jetsam was still commenting:

"The dog hyar next to the *D* hain't so good. Don't look like a feisty bitin' one. But this hyar hat. Why hit's the spittin' image o' Lazer Gardner's hat. Seen it a hundred times."

Praise is sweet—all the sweeter for being reluctant praise. Dencey began to brighten.

"An' the letters—all in a row. Why, it's as good as a ship's list. Ye kin tell the hull cargo."

But even without the ship's list, Jetsam had done admirably. He remembered every word, seeing it on the page, and even spelled many from memory. Dionis, accustomed to the baby minds she taught at school, was delighted at this progress—a fleet chase with which she could hardly keep up.

"An' now I know all o' them. Ef I could just write 'em."
How he grasped at the book with both hands as if it might
fly away from him. "Would ye show me the writin'?" he
asked wistfully.

"But I didn't promise to teach thee to write," said Dionis
the Just.

"No," he said. He paused, measuring her shrewdly. He
was baffled. "Then I must just git it my own self."

The book, her precious *Pilgrim's Progress,* had greatly
degenerated. Greasy where his hands had gripped it,
wrinkled and stained.

"Why, Sam Jetsam!" spoke out Dencey. "I'd think thee'd
be ashamed. Thee's torn another page—no, two more."

"I didn't do that." His face went instantly white and
hard. Dencey had a flashing remembrance of the day she
threw the stone. "Injun Jill done that." Here an angry oath.
"I was studyin' by the firelight, an' she comes up an'
snatches afore I kin git hold. She run to the other side o'
the room. Lordy, I thought hit was a goner. I never could
git nothin' back off her. But I got this book. I kicked her
an' bit her. She'll remember it, I reckon."

"What did she want?" asked Dencey, puzzled. "Did she
read it herself?"

"Her! She can't read no more'n a cat. An' she says, if
she can't, I sha'n't. I sha'n't be no better'n what she is."

"But thee is better, anyway."

Dionis had no idea beforehand of making such an as-
sertion. It burst out along with her indignation and pity.

As for Jetsam, he gave two assenting grunts, Indian
fashion. Then he sat still, staring into space.

"Well, go on," said Dencey, who was always steering
back to the main course. " 'Then Christian fell down'— If

thee learns three more words it'll be a sentence."

Somehow, Jetsam was very hoarse on those three words.

So the lessons multiplied in the old Brown barn. Soon Jetsam could read whole sentences, haltingly and with abominable inflections. Yet he read them. Then, suddenly, he acquired a marvelous swiftness, and Dencey discovered he was saying it by heart. With scathing reprimand, she skipped him over to the end of the book. The thing was to be done right!

And there were lessons other than the reading, lessons of which both children were quite unaware. Jetsam lost his temper at every mistake and then swore oaths, various and picturesque—the gleanings from the docks and shipyards.

"I don't think," remarked Dencey, "that thee should speak of Jesus that way."

"Why not?" he demanded, his finger still on the sentence which had tripped him up.

"I think it might hurt His feelings."

"His feelin's! What ye mean? Jesus—hit's jist a word ye say."

"A word!" Nothing could exceed the scorn and horror. "Thee knows better than that, Sam Jetsam. Thee isn't a Fiji or a Chinaman."

Jetsam squirmed.

"Well, sayin' 'Jesus', hit's jist like sayin' 'God.' I reckon He don't hyar it."

"He hears everything, Jesus does," declared the Quaker Dencey. "Why, He hears thy thoughts. And—and He talks too. He talks to Mother when she stays alone in her room. He doesn't talk to Grandfather, 'cause he's a Congregationalist. But Aunt Lovesta, why He tells her to go places, an' she goes. She saw Him once, Aunt Lovesta did."

Jetsam was thoroughly scared.

"He hain't on Nantucket, is He?" he inquired.

"Of course He's on Nantucket. Why, Aunt Lovesta says He even goes to the Fijis' land, only they don't know it. He wouldn't leave out Nantucket! Well, I guess not!"

The next time Jetsam took the name of his Lord in vain, his tongue clove to the roof of his mouth.

16. *The Beloved Aunt Lovesta*

O F COURSE, DIONIS could not have accomplished all these visits and absences had it not been for Aunt Lovesta Coffyn.

Aunt Lovesta lived on Mill Street, and Dencey's custom had been to go to see her almost every day. Thus, between the two places, Dencey's flittings were not noticed.

Lovesta Coffyn was as different from Lydia as day from night. Yet she also was Quakeress to the core. Perhaps even more typical Quakeress than Lydia, though people of Lovesta's power are not common in any sect or city.

When the little girl entered the room, Aunt Lovesta would greet her with a warmth that was like a kiss. Of course, she did not kiss her, for that was not Quaker custom.

"And how is thee to-day?" would say her deep large voice. "I know thee got that sum. Ciphering couldn't get ahead of thee. Now, could it?"

"No, I got it right—as good as Hopestill. And this morning I spelled down everybody, even Caleb Folger.

And he can spell *representation* and *indescribable* and never gets mixed in the endings. That isn't worldly boastings, is it, Aunt Lovesta? 'Cause it's true."

Here would follow some long meaningless tale that children love to narrate, and Aunt Lovesta would listen to the very end. In the brightness of this shining, Dencey would unfold and expand—laugh softly as she chattered. Never did Lydia know the inadvertent confessions, the childish puzzlements and terrors which all came to Aunt Lovesta.

Did Lydia suspect this? She seldom refused that oft-repeated request, "Mother, may I go to Aunt Lovesta's?" Yet, as she said her "Yes," her lips pressed into a straight line which spoiled the beauty of her mouth.

Aunt Lovesta was tall and full of health. Coming toward you (and she always did that) she moved serene and alive, like a full-sailed ship. Her garments seemed always to sweep backward, though she did not walk fast. Benevolence beamed from her eyes, and from her face an enviable happiness. The Quaker gray of her dress, her kerchief white as mist, seemed only to throw into relief something colorful and flamboyant within her.

Aunt Lovesta was a preacher and had her "minute" to go upon religious journeys to speak the word of life. She would suddenly be "under concern" to go to South Carolina, up the Hudson, or into Canada—wherever the Spirit led. Dionis would come to her home to find her shawled and bonneted, her carpet bag in her hand, starting away to the "packet."

"Oh, Aunt Lovesta, take me with thee on thy errand for God," she would plead.

"There are too many dangers for a little girl," Aunt

Lovesta would answer. "When thee grows up, perhaps the Lord will send thee on errands of thy own!"

And Dionis, with a little bleakness and a little fear, would think how the Lord had never yet spoken to her. Perhaps He never would!

Aunt Lovesta was the soul of trustfulness. Thus, when Dencey, flush-faced, would come in after school and at the end of a few moments would start up again, Aunt Lovesta was miles away from any suspicion.

"What, going home so soon?" she would query. "I only get a glimpse of thee these days."

"Yes," Dencey would reply, with eyes looking somewhere else. "I have to go."

"Here take a fresh doughnut, child. Does thee feel quite well?"

"Yes, I'm well. Fare thee well, Aunt Lovesta."

And Dencey would speed away toward the Commons and Brown's barn, wondering, "Was it a lie? I didn't say I was goin' home. But I said 'yes.' I guess 'yes' is a lie."

A lie to Aunt Lovesta. What would Aunt Lovesta think of Dencey if she knew? There was cold isolation as the curtain of her lie slid softly down between Dencey and those she loved.

17. *The Adventure of the Coat*

AND BESIDES THE lies, there was stealing!
Dionis called it just that. Quakers are not apt to call
things by covered-up names. It began with the stealing of
Stephen's coat.

Dencey was sitting in the kitchen corner washing the
crude salt when Stephen came flinging in.

"I won't wear this coat once more—not once. Look at
the rags dangling."

He snatched the coat off and threw it on the floor.

"Thee can't waste a coat like that, Stephen Severance,"
declared Peggy. "It does perfectly well for bringing in the
wood."

"It doesn't. Besides, I've got Uncle Tom's old coat for
that. There goes!"

He gave the coat a kick. Of course, Lydia was not within
hearing of such independence.

Dencey, in her corner, was visited by an unexpected
flash: *If Jetsam had that coat!*

It would cover up that space of dirty white skin she
could always see on Jetsam's chest. Yes, and the hole in

the back showing some vertebræ. Dencey didn't like these glimpses.

"Thee's a fool, Stephen," Peggy was saying. "Throwin' away a coat just 'cause Hannah Bourne seen thee in it, over the fence. Even if thee is soft on Hannah—"

"I'm not soft on Hannah," retorted the crimson-faced Stephen. "But I won't wear rags, Peg Runnel."

(*If Jetsam had that coat.* If he only had it. Peggy was hanging it on a hook and laughing at Stephen. But, of course, Jetsam couldn't have it. Dencey would never dare to ask Mother or even Stephen about it.)

But all day the thought dragged at her like a child at her skirts. In school and on her way home.

If Jetsam had that coat. He hasn't got one at all. Only that pea-jacket for rain! And Jill wears that most rains. He just wears his shirt. The same shirt always, always.

That night she was undressing alone by the embers of the kitchen fire. She wasn't thinking about the coat at all. When, presto, there it was, where the devil himself had prepared it, stuffed behind the kitchen wood-box in a tight roll.

With sudden impulse, Dencey snatched it and ran upstairs to her room. Of course, she wouldn't give it to Jetsam. She knew she wouldn't do that. But why did her heart pound so?

Mother had once said, "Dencey, when thee has done wrong, Something always tells thee. God leaves no one without the Inner Guiding Light. Thee will know!"

Yes, she knew. It was a damnable deed. She would not steal Stephen's coat; she'd slip downstairs, after a while, when everybody was asleep, and put it back where Stephen had hidden it. But between this action and the doing of it swam always the picture of Jetsam with the thin torn shirt—sometimes plastered flat to his body by the rain. Ugh!

She did not go downstairs. She lay awake hour after hour. She was a thief. She would go to hell. Mother didn't say so. But Grandfather did—and that it was burning forever.

Still she could not take the coat downstairs to its place again.

She sat up in bed, cold with perspiration on her forehead. There was the moon rising over the dim sea—the sea which moved in the darkness and whispered. Father was on that sea somewhere far and far. If he knew he had a thief for a daughter, what would he do?

At the thought of Father, she began to cry softly.

Still she did not take the coat downstairs to its place.

Difficulties next day, oh, many of them. The taking the coat to school in a bundle, the hiding it with her coat. Then taking it out to Brown's barn, always, even yet, saying to herself that she would not give the coat to Jetsam. But the day was rainy—cold as, in Nantucket, a northeaster in June can be cold! Jetsam, as he settled himself beside her on the hay, was plainly shivering.

Dencey suddenly thrust the bundle at him.

"Here, Sam Jetsam," she said roughly. "Thee take that. It's a coat."

There were unexpected outcroppings of pride in Jetsam.

"It hain't my coat," he said. "Why should I take it?"

"Because thee's cold. Put it on, I say."

"I hain't cold. I've got enough on."

"Thee hasn't, Sam Jetsam. I can see thy skin in three places. It isn't right," she burst forth with sudden Quaker justice, "for one boy to have three coats and another not even one."

"Who's got three coats?"

"Why, Stephen. And he threw this one away."

Jetsam opened the bundle. Reluctantly he put his arms in both armholes at once, drew the coat on over his head, boy way, settled into it snugly.

"H'm!" he grunted. "Steve hadn't oughta throwd a coat like this away."

And Dencey, looking at him, felt strangely, suddenly warm. As if she herself had put on the coat.

18. *More Adventure of the Coat*

DENCEY STOOD ONE day in the corner of Aunt Lovesta's keeping room. Stood and stood.

"What does thee want, child?" asked her aunt. "Come here, let me feel thy cheek. Why is thee so hot?"

Denecy came unwillingly.

"Aunt Lovesta," she asked, "does a thief always go to hell?"

"Why, what put such a question in thy head, Dencey?"

"I—I just want to know. Does he?"

"No, child. If he is sorry, if he repents truly, he does not—even a thief."

"What is repenting truly?"

Aunt Lovesta was pleased. Lydia had always called Dencey an unspiritual child, but what searching questions, these.

"Repenting truly is feeling so sorry to the dear Lord that thee is sure thee will never do it again."

Dencey fetched a deep sigh.

"But suppose the—the man is sure he will do it again."

"Then, dear child, he has not repented."

"And—and if he doesn't repent he will go to hell." Dencey's eyes were wide and dark and a little wild.

"Dear child, fix not thy thought on hell, but in the inward and spiritual light. That will guide thee and tell thee all. Does thee know somebody who has stolen something?"

"No—oh, no," hastened the startled Dencey. "I was just thinking. Grandfather was—was telling me about the sin against the Holy Ghost."

Aunt Lovesta's black eyes snapped with displeasure. Lydia must somehow prevent the old man from teaching the child false doctrine.

"Stealing is not the unforgivable sin. We have Scripture for that, Dencey. Does thee not remember what our Lord said to the thief on the cross—'To-day thou shalt be with me in Paradise'?"

Aunt Lovesta's face began to glow with her "preaching look."

"Had the thief on the cross repented?" asked the persistent Dencey.

"Yes, child."

"But how could He know he had? Why, he wouldn't ever have a chance to steal again, Aunt Lovesta. Maybe Christ was just sorry for him and forgave him anyways."

"No, no. Our Lord is not lax. The thief had repented. Make sure of that, Dencey."

Already Aunt Lovesta was unconsciously dreaming of this for a next First Day talk. She was not as keen as she might have been to search to the bottom of Dencey's fear.

Dencey went off more miserable than ever. Could she stop stealing food for Jetsam? Would she take the warm coat from Jetsam and give it back to Stephen who had three? No, she had not repented, and without repentance there was no hope.

But the matter of the coat was not to remain an inner conflict in the bosom of Dencey Coffyn.

The loss of a coat with four good buttons and half a yard of unbroken cloth could hardly go unnoted in a Quaker household. Dencey, coming into the kitchen, found her mother and Peggy in serious conversation.

"I hung it on a peg near the hearth," said Peggy with a hurt sniff. "And that's the plum last I seen on't."

"Now, Peggy, I don't suspect thee, so there's no use sniffing," said Lydia, her hands pushing strongly at the bread dough. "Stephen must have made away with it as he said he would. There was plenty stuff to make over for Barna's trousers. Agatha Mitchell wove it, and she beats her cloth so firm that it lasts forever.—There, now, I don't mean that." Lydia corrected herself, Quaker fashion. "But Mother's dress of her weaving lasted twenty years."

At this juncture, who should come in but Stephen himself. Lydia began at once.

"Stephen, thee must remember about the coat. Where has thee got it?"

"I haven't got it, Aunt Lydia. I told thee I did stuff it down behind the wood-box just for a joke. But I can't find it now."

"Well, it's very strange," persisted Lydia, whose understanding of boys was none of the best. "Peggy has searched and I—"

"Look here, Aunt Lydia!" Stephen's nice face darkened. "I've never lied to thee and I'm not lying now!" His eyes blinked, and he banged down his school books and hurried out.

If anyone had glanced at Dionis, the truth must have been known at once. She stood with lips apart and eyes shadowed with horror.

Stephen under a cloud for her fault. Why, Stephen was crying—big Stephen!

She was on the point of speaking out, confessing all. How easy to say, "I took the coat. I gave it to Sammie Jetsam." The reproof, how easy to bear. The whipping, how light a thing compared to the horror of this guilt.

But then there was Mother's astonishment to be reckoned with. "What, thee gave the coat to Sammie Jetsam? What in the world was thee doing with Sammie Jetsam, and on the Commons too!" Mother would not only take away the coat, but all Sammie's lessons as well. Dencey's ideas about the whole matter were as unheroic as might be. She knew only that she was teaching Sammie to read *Pilgrim's Progress* and giving him something to eat now and then.

But back of all this concreteness was the curious cognizance of childhood. Dencey knew with an intensity that equalled its vagueness that if she let go of Jetsam, he would tumble back into an abyss. Hatred, abuse, filthy talk, and fear—all these were in it; and she alone held him back from the lip of it.

This thing clutched her with such power that she could not speak. Not even now.

She slunk like a cat out of the door and went through the back gate down to the beach.

This time she did not weep softly but with actual sobbing.

But still Dencey did not tell about the coat.

19. *The Adventure of the Book*

"LOOKY HYAR," SAID Jetsam as they closed *Pilgrim's Progress* for the day. "Ef I tell ye suthin', will ye cross yer heart not to tell?"

"I don't make vain oaths," said the Quaker Dencey. "What does thee want to tell, anyway?"

"But will ye tell it?"

"No, o' course not."

"Ye know how Injun Jill she tried to git my book. Well, thet night I hid it in the wood-pile outside. An' in the middle o' the night I woke up and thar was Injun Jill a-pokin' around the cabin with a ole can'el. She'd felt under my bed, an' thet's what woke me. Ye see, my bed's jist a bag o' shucks on the floor."

"Did she find it?" asked Dencey, breathless.

"No, she didn't. She got hot, though. After she'd poked around into all the corners, she went out into the wood-shed. I follered, creepin' on my hands and knees. But hit was awful windy, an' the wind blew out the can'el, an' she swore an' come back. I tell ye I hed to make a skip an' a hop back on to my bed and pretend to snore."

Jetsam chuckled. Evidently this tale had a happy ending.

"An' that mornin' at sun-up, I got up and took my book—" As Jetsam said this a small unconscious gesture of the grimy boy hand passed sofly over the leather cover— "Well, I hid it somewhar else. Hit's a good place, too."

"Where is it?" Dencey leaned forward intensely with her question.

"I wun't tell ye."

"Thee said thee'd tell me. Please, Jetsam."

"Ye'd go an' tell. Girls allus do."

"Girls don't." Dencey flushed with indignation. "Hopestill and me, we have secrets an' we never tell, never, never."

"Hum-um," he grunted negatively. "I know. Ye'd git mad sometime and then ye'd tell."

"I'm mad now," she declared. "But I wouldn't tell. Thee's mean, Sam Jetsam, that's what thee is."

But no threats nor anger moved him. His face screwed up into Yankee shrewdness.

"A secret's best with jist one," he asserted. "An' that one's goin' to be me."

All the way home, Dencey's indignant thoughts were on the book—that treasure hidden away like Captain Kidd's gold on Gardiner's Island. How mean of Jetsam not to tell her. If she only knew the snug hiding place and could fetch it out in defiance of Injun Jill, as Jetsam did every day.

There came a sou'wester to Nantucket—water from above pouring in sheets, water all about in great breakers lashing the beaches. The little island seemed sinking and dissolving into its vast home. The very air was salt and could be tasted on the lips.

After this, it was to be observed that the long-suffering volume of *Pilgrim* was covered with blue mold.

"Hit was gittin' wet," acknowledged Jetsam. "But it wun't no more. I got a box yest'd'y—a wooden box, good an' tight. I traded it off a sailor fur a hull baskit o' clams. The box came from Inja an's got heathen pictures all over it. I wrapped the book in a shirt an' put it in the box—whar, I wun't tell ye."

But the very next day he had to tell her everything.

He came to the lesson with his eyes snapping with excitement.

"She almost got it," he cried. "She almost did. I was jist hidin' the box in its hole—"

"What hole?" asked Dencey slyly.

"Oh, in the side o' a bank right near our passel o' woods. Thar's a juniper hangs all over hit like a closed hatch. I was puttin' it in thar when I heard suthin'—ye know a cat can't go no softer than her—an' thar, less'n a cable's length away, was Injun Jill, plain as a lighthus."

"What did thee do? What did thee do?" cried Dencey.

"She did fust. 'I got ye,' she yells, an' makes a dash. But I was too quick fer her," boasted the boy. "I grabbed the box an' skipped—like a brig in a gale. The cargo was heavy too. Injun Jill, she like to 'a' caught me. But she wus swearin' so hard an' so tarnal mad she wa'n't lookin' good—an' her foot caught, it did, an' down she went. 'Fore she got up, I was out o' sight behind the woods."

"Oh," breathed Dencey. She saw the blissful terror of the scene. Jetsam running with the heavy box. Injun Jill so swift after him—the wicked cruelty of her face.

She beat her hands upon her lap in fine impatience.

"What will thee do?" she queried. "What'll thee do now, Sam Jetsam?"

"I dunno what," he answered blankly.

"Thee'll have to do something quick."

In a strange instant all Jetsam's boasting was gone. The terror of Injun Jill came back upon him.

"They hain't no use to hide it. She'll find it anyways, she will."

Dencey could not understand the change.

"Why, no, she can't," she declared. "We can hide it the other side of town—'way down by Brant Point, if we want to."

In the boy's face was something more than fear. Bafflement, a curious hurt, as if he were a sensitive girl instead of the hard little waif he was. At such times his face went perfectly white and his cheek bones stood out prominently.

"Injun Jill, she says I cain't larn to read."

"But thee reads now."

"I read like hell," he answered roughly. "Injun Jill, she kep' at me all night sayin' I cain't beat her, hidin' my book, 'cause she's Indian smart an' I'm only half Indian. She said nasty things about the white man that wus my pap. She says I'm jist trash."

Dencey swept to the rescue as if with a banner.

"Thee isn't trash, Sam Jetsam. Thee studies harder than any boy in the Coffin School. Thee learns quick as lightnin'."

He looked up into her face—not hoping—only listening.

Dencey sprang up and stamped her foot angrily.

"Thee's a 'fraid-cat, Sam Jetsam. Come along out o' the barn. I'm going to hide the book myself."

Surprising, but Jetsam got up obediently and followed her. She led the way over the wide Commons, now by little sheep paths, now striking straight across among the low huckleberries and mealy-plum. Apparently, she knew exactly where she was going. From a hilltop spread the gray infinity of sea.

"Hurry," she said.

They scrambled down the bank and through the high spear grass, to the white pure beach, desolate, untouched. The only sign that life had ever been there was the wreck of a ketch, dismasted and half buried in the sand.

"We'll hide it in the ketch," said Dencey breathlessly. "We can put the box down in the hold."

Jetsam had by this time caught the spark.

"No, I'll tell ye," he answered. "The ketch has got a bowsprit—part o' one, anyways. We'll use that for a sighter. Here, ye take the box and I'll go to the ketch an' sight along her bowsprit. An' when ye comes to the spot the bowsprit pints to, I'll sing out, an' ye stop."

He ran to the wreck and, lying flat on the deck, squinted along the spar.

"Port," he shouted. "Starboard—starboard agin. Halt—lay to."

Now all breathless, he joined Dencey. They began to dig in the sand as if life depended on it. Dencey with bare hands, and Jetsam with a stick he had brought from the ketch.

"This place is above spring tide even," he said. "See all the spear grass?"

"But can we find it really when we want it?"

"'Course we kin. Nothin's sure as sightin'."

For once Dencey forgot the lesson. The hiding of the

treasure possessed her mind. As they dug, the sea kept up its whispering, pouring sound. Far out on the gray, a loon called—a wild pure note like the ultimate expression of solitude.

Dencey stood up, straightened her back, and looked down the length of the Island. Seen thus along the edge, the shore seemed to stretch endlessly, cape after cape— then beach, then cape again, and the white lips of the sea gravely touching it, and the mist stealing in over the water.

"We can't see Tuckernuck to-day," she said dreamily.

What satisfaction to know that the book was safe at last. The children did not question why Injun Jill wanted it. They only knew she mustn't get it. They knew somehow that Jetsam's escape lay in that hidden treasure.

20. *Injun Jill Knows*

THERE IS A SAYING which begins, "If looks could kill." It implies that looks cannot kill, and like most wise saws, it is not true. The looks which Injun Jill was casting over toward Sammie Jetsam were effectually killing any tenderness or trust which might be in the boy's character.

They were shut in the little cottage. Jetsam was pretending not to see her as he crouched low against the smouldering hearth. But he was watching Injun Jill with furtive misery.

"Awful smard hidin' fro' Indion Jeel," she murmured in the Nantucket Indian jargon he knew so well. "Go many blaces but Indion Jeel knowth all blaces—she knowth all times."

Sam did not answer but began raking the embers together for warmth and light.

"Ye say, 'me go into down.' Nobody seen ye on docks yesdy. Nobody seen ye in down, an' Sammie 'way all tay."

This seemed a great joke, for Indian Jill tittered and chuckled as she began to bang her loom. Every bang seemed to hit Jetsam with a new fear. How often in his babyhood that banging had stopped suddenly to give him an unexpected blow. He looked away. What did she know? What would she say next?

"Whar wus ye?" she demanded.

Only silence.

"Ye answer me. I kin peat ye yet, Sam Jeshum."

This was true. Injun Jill's strength was that of some sturdy pony—little and bent though she was.

"Fishin'," said Sam.

"Whar's the feesh?"

"Didn't ketch none."

"Liar. Lyin' scoundrelth. Jest like white daddy. Think ye're petter nor Indion Jeel. Oh, lots petter."

Oh, the scorn of this. The bitterness of those little beady eyes. The bitterness in the very air of the cottage. All the outward aspect of the place—its age-old untidiness, dirt and rags in corners, two little windows so caked with dust that only a faint gray light came through—the low closed-in-ness—the abominable smell—all these were but the showing of that inward bitterness that dwelt there and flourished its thorny life.

With a half-sob the boy sprang up and flung himself toward the door.

"Bring wood, ye slaggard," rasped Injun Jill's voice after him. And it showed the hag's ascendancy over him that the boy did bring the wood and threw his thunderous armful on the hearth.

When he had been a tiny babe, this authority of Injun Jill had set its clutches deep into his spirit. Had some courage in him been killed then? He had no strength to loose that hold.

As he sat again upon the hearth, Injun Jill came leaning over him. He flung up his arm to ward off her blow, but she did not cuff him. Instead she said:

"Ye goeth Prown barn, Sam Jeshum. I watch ye. That leetle minx, Dence Coff'n, she go all blaces wit ye."

Sam sprang up, backing away and whimpering.

"Hi, hi, yi, thet skeerth ye, does it? Indion Jeel watch once." She told it off with her fingers. "Indion Jeel watch dwo dimes, Indion Jeel *ketch!*"

She turned her back and trudged over to the loom shaking with laughter.

"Dence Coff'n, Dence Coff'n," she crooned, "Indion Jeel ketch. Then Dence Coff'n nobody see anny more."

21. *The Adventure of Dencey*

IT WAS A STRANGE and wild-eyed Jetsam that Dencey discovered next day sitting in the sand by the old ketch.

"Couldn't thee find the book?" she asked anxiously.

"I hain't tried."

"But thee must try. We must get our lesson. We didn't have it yesterday."

He kept looking straight in front of him, not at Dencey.

"Injun Jill don't want the book no more," he said dully.

"Then we needn't hide it any more?" Dencey was plainly disappointed. But he did not hear her.

"Hit's you, Dencey Coffyn," he announced, turning suddenly upon her. "Hit's you she wants."

"Me? Injun Jill?"

Jetsam nodded. Dencey's healthy tan faded to a gray.

"What for?" she whispered.

"'Cause ye teaches me to read. She says nobody sha'n't teach me but her. Her teach!" His upper lip curled back in scorn.

"What'll she do?" gasped Dencey.

"Beat ye! Beat ye tell ye can't stand up. That's what she does to me." Jetsam paused, then said with that fatalism which always beset him:

"She says she'll ketch ye. An' if she says it, she'll do it."

The two children stared at each other, too frightened to plan.

"An' now," the boy went on, "now ye won't come no more."

Dencey stood breathing hard.

"Ye'd better go quick," he advised.

"Yes," she answered.

Then she turned and half ran along the beach toward home.

She glanced back. Jetsam sat just as she had left him, staring out over the water—a small figure there on the wide desolate beach—waiting. Waiting for what? For Injun Jill. There was nothing else for him to wait for. Only Injun Jill.

Dencey's going began to be slower—slower. Her feet seemed weighted. Never had the sand been so deep, so sifty.

She looked back again.

New England Responsibility! Eight generations had bred it into Dencey Coffyn. It had begun long ago in the New England faith in immortality—their vivid sense of their unending life. They were responsible for their own immortal souls, responsible for the town, responsible for the state.

The dynamic of the old New Englander's responsibility still lives and keeps the decency of our American cities. No wonder it could weight the feet of one little girl running away.

Dencey stopped. She turned about, stared at Jetsam's huddled figure, now a speck in the lonely distance. And with a little sob, half for him, half for herself, Dencey started back.

Her head was down. She walked swiftly along the beach, not looking.

Suddenly Jetsam was beside her, breathless from running.

Fool and blind, he did not notice that Dencey was coming, not going. Fool and blind, he blurted out the purpose with which he had sprung up to run after her.

"Come back," he shouted. "Ye've got to. I hain't forgive ye, I tell ye. I hain't forgive ye yit."

Dencey stopped short. Her anger blazed, a sudden fire.

She had been coming back to him, and he—he could say this mean and ugly threat. Her pity, her kindness, her purpose, all swept into the burning.

"Sam Jetsam," she sobbed. "Thee is a mean, mean, *mean* despiseable boy. I won't come back. If thee can't forgive me, thee needn't. I don't care. I don't care one bit."

Jetsam had a sudden inkling that he had done some mischief. He had more than an inkling that his hold on Dencey Coffyn was completely gone.

He began to follow after her, aimless, puzzled, frightened. As for Dencey, she was fairly running from him.

"Come back," he insisted. "I don't want ye to go."

She pushed on, head down.

"We kin fight Injun Jill—the both of us. I'll knock her down an' ye can kick her."

Dencey shuddered, still hurrying.

"I'll fight her myself. Say, I won't let her hurt ye."

No use. A light was slowly dawning in Jetsam's mind.

"Say," he faltered at last. "I didn't mean that thar about not forgivin' ye. I allus did forgive ye. Please come back."

Dencey paused.

"I was comin'," she asserted. "I won't now."

"Ye wus comin'?" Jetsam was blankly astonished.

"Yes, looky there, my tracks. I'd gone 'way up there to that rock."

Sure enough, there were the two sets of stubby footprints—the going ones and the coming ones.

Jetsam was fearfully puzzled. Why had she come back if she didn't care for the forgiveness? Why had she run away again at his threat? Why did it frighten him so not to understand it? And now, all of a sudden, he didn't want her to come back and get hurt by Injun Jill. Gee Whillikins, he was going to cry! Why, even Injun Jill couldn't make him cry these days.

All the time, he dug one toe into the sand, breathing short and hard and saying nothing.

"Well, Sam Jetsam, if thee doesn't want me, I can go home. I'd lots rather, anyway."

Dencey's voice broke in upon the miserable shadows and woke him up.

" 'Course I want ye," he said roughly. "Ye come along."

22. *Injun Jill Pursues*

"YE KIN DO THE sightin'," Jetsam said generously as they came to the ketch. And Dencey, greatly honored, lay on the old rotten deck squinting along the bowsprit. She did not "sight" so accurately as Jetsam, but finally the lacquered box was found and the book lifted out. Then the two sat down together on the sand.

They were come to an unfortunate chapter—

"'And in the midst of the valley I perceived the mouth of hell to be, and ever and anon flame and smoke would come out in such abundance. . . .Also he heard doleful voices and rushings to and fro. Christian resolved to go on. Yet the fiends seemed to come nearer and nearer.'"

The children were ill at ease. Jetsam kept glancing behind him as he read. Dencey steadfastly kept her eyes on the text. But her finger trembled, following the lines.

"'Just as he was come over against the mouth of the pit, one of the wicked ones gat behind him, and whisperingly suggested grievous blasphemies to him.'"

This was too much. Both children looked behind at once. Jetsam forgot to read. Dencey jumped to her feet and began fishing in the folds of her dress for her pocket.

"I—I forgot something." She gasped a little as she spoke. "It's writing—so thee can learn to write. I stol—took it out of a barrel in the attic."

She opened it, glad of the activity.

"Did ye write it?"

"No. It's a sermon. Uncle Hubert's. He died years an' years ago."

She read the title.

" 'The Sin of Marrying a Deceased Wife's Sister.' "

"What's that?" queried Jetsam. "What kind of a sister is that?"

"I don't know, only this says it's a sin to marry her."

"Well, who'd marry his sister anyways? That's silly."

"No, it isn't. It's a Congregationalist sermon. Thee mustn't call a sermon silly."

The argument did them good. They began to read the book again, choosing another place.

" 'And in that town there is a fair kept called Vanity Fair. Beelzebub, Apollyon, and Legion contrived that it should last all the year long. Therefore at this fair are all such merchandise sold as houses, trades, honors, titles, delights of all sorts, bodies, souls, silver, gold, precious stones and what not.' "

Jetsam looked up with shining eyes.

"Whar d'ye s'pose that town is?" he asked.

"Well, it isn't in Nantucket," declared Dencey. "It must

be on the Main."

"I'm goin' to ask some o' the sailors about that thar port," he said. "They'll know it, shore." He bent quickly to the book again.

" 'And moreover at this Fair is to be seen juggling, cheats, games, plays, fools, apes, knaves, and that of every kind. Here are to be seen and that for nothing, thefts, murders, false swears and that of a blood-red color.' "

"Lordy," he breathed. "I whisht I could go thar."

Dencey was properly horrified.

"Why, Sam Jetsam, thee mustn't wish that. That's light and worldly pleasures. And look who's head of the Fair, Beelzebub and Apollyon."

"I don't keer, I'm goin' to see it some day. 'A false-swearer and that of a blood-red color,' " he mused. "An' monkeys, Lordy!"

"But, Jetsam, look here, when thee reads further—"

But they did not read further. A shadow fell suddenly across the page.

There was Injun Jill—the foul fiend herself—grinning and terrible.

With one shriek the children scattered. Injun Jill's quick grab at them met the empty air. She had been so sure of her prey that at the miss she stumbled forward. This gave them time. They scampered. They fairly flew over the sand. Jetsam clasped the book. Dencey lifted her great bundle of skirts in both hands and actually kept up with Jetsam. Terror gave her wings. It was herself Injun Jill was after. Herself and no other.

They scrambled up the bank and began to run over the

rough Commons. Injun Jill's head appeared above the bank just behind them.

"Hi, I git ye," she triumphed. "I ketch—Whoo!"

On they ran. Here, in the tangle of huckleberry, Injun Jill had the advantage.

Once Dencey tripped on a blackberry brier, but with a mounting prayer was up again.

But Injun Jill was gaining. She was almost upon them. It would be only a moment more, and then—

Suddenly Jetsam shoved against her. He thrust the book into her hand.

"Hyar, take it!" he gasped.

Even amid their running, Dencey saw the meanness of the deed. He was giving her the book so he could run light and get away. She clasped it mechanically amid her skirts and was sharply aware of a stitch in her side. Oh, could she run any more?

"No—thet way. Thet way!" Jetsam screamed, pointing to the town. "Not with me!"

He disappeared. She ran as he had pointed. It was his purpose pushed her. She did not know where she was going. She ran pelting, panting, exhausted, the book in her arms.

But now she no longer heard Injun Jill behind her.

She glanced back.

There was Jetsam quite far away right in front of Injun Jill. Now he dodged under her elbow, so she whirled about in fury. But he had dodged quite another way. Injun Jill, bewildered by her scattered enemies, started toward Dencey. Jetsam yelled some taunt at her, and she started toward him again.

Ah, he was far away over the Commons.

A light broke upon Dencey.

Jetsam had run back to save her. He had run almost into Injun Jill's arms.

23. *The Promise*

ALL NIGHT LONG Dionis puzzled over her problem. How could she ever meet Jetsam again?

She could not go to Brown's barn. Injun Jill knew that place. Not to the old ketch—surely! Could she go out into the Commons and just wait? With the chance that Injun Jill would find her and destroy?

Meanwhile, she had the *Pilgrim's Progress*. This was worst of all. What would Jetsam do without it? How could she ever get it to him?

Trudging to school next morning she thought and thought about it. Coming home, she thought again. Then, suddenly, there was no need to think about it any more.

Her mother met her at the kitchen door, stern, white, and silent. She led her upstairs and into "Mother's Room." She closed the door. Then—

"Dionis, is it true thee went out to Brown's barn and met that boy called Jetsam?"

The doom had sounded like a solemn bell. "Mother's Room" looked queer, as if Dionis had never seen it before. The awful silence! It did not occur to Dencey to speak.

125

"Answer me, Dionis."

"Mother," she gasped, "how did thee know?"

"Never mind. Oh, does that mean that thee did?" Lydia's voice broke with agitation.

"Yes, Mother—at Brown's barn and on the beach, too."

"Oh, then Injun Jill was right. I thought she was only crazy."

Lydia's face whitened. The child would be branded as a bad little girl. Lydia herself would be blamed for not keeping better watch. The Committee on Sufferings would come and publicly reprimand her.

"Child," she faltered, "why did thee do it?"

"I had to go."

"Had to! Nonsense! Doesn't thee know he is the worst boy in the whole town? No respectable boys will play with him. But thee—a nice little girl!"

Dencey looked up, catching the scare.

"He swears," she said doubtfully. "He says awful things about our Lord."

"But didn't that offend thee?"

"Yes. I—I made him stop. But he does it again."

Lydia held her daughter's arm trembling. Injun Jill had said dreadful things about Lydia's little girl. She had appeared suddenly at the kitchen door and said them. Right before Peggy, too.

"What did you play together? Tell me. Did he touch thee?"

"Touch me? Why, Mother. He wouldn't want to. An' his hands are just black. An' he won't wash at all, 'cepting in the sea."

Lydia breathed relief. She dropped Dencey's arm.

"And thee always tells the truth, child. That I know."

"No, I don't," Dencey answered. "Oh, Mother, I've lied and lied to thee."

Suddenly a great lot of ripples started up and down Dencey's throat. She couldn't swallow them. It was because she was glad. This whole encounter changed for her in a moment, in the twinkling of an eye. It wasn't a calamity. It was a relief, a rescue, the thing she had longed for, for ages. Now she could tell all—sweep the decks clear.

"Yes, I lied to thee," she sobbed. "An' I stole too. It was me took Steve's coat, an' I lied about it. An' I took bread an' cake an' things an' gave 'em to Jetsam. He was so hungry. And, oh, Mother, will I go to hell?"

Aunt Lovesta would have gathered the little girl in her arms. She would by small tender encouragements have got the whole story. Lydia was frozen. Fear for her child swept her. If Dencey lied, how could Lydia ever exonerate her?

"Dionis—oh, I thought I had brought thee up in the fear of the Lord. Thee has been stealing, thee says, and lying to me. Why did thee lie? I have never whipped thee nor made thee afraid. It was cruel to treat me like that. Oh, if thy father were only here!"

Miserable was Dencey at this outburst from her mother. The sin had evidently been worse than Dencey had imagined. Surely Mother had some remedy.

"Couldn't Grandfather whip me?" she suggested. "Wouldn't that help?"

"No, it will only help for thee to stop lying, stop stealing, stop touching the pitch and playing with that boy who swears and curses his God."

"But I wasn't playing, Mother."

"What was thee doing, then? Do speak out."

"I was teaching him to read," Dencey faltered.

Lydia leaned toward her, puzzled yet eager.

"Teaching him? Child, however did thee happen to do that? Is thee telling the truth?"

"Oh, yes, Mother," Dencey sobbed suddenly. "I won't lie to thee now. "I'll—I'll never lie to thee again."

Lydia took Dencey's hands. Two big tears rolled down her cheeks.

"I believe thee, Dionis," she said. "Now, how did thee happen to teach him?"

"Because he wouldn't forgive me."

"Forgive thee! For what?"

Could it be that Mother had forgotten that Judgment Day when the heavens rolled up as a scroll?

"Why, Mother, for hitting him with a stone. And thee couldn't go with me because of Martha White, an' I went, an' he broke my ammonite shell, an'—an' I gave him *Pilgrim's Progress*, an' then he wouldn't forgive me until I'd teach him. An' I taught him an' taught him. He learns quick. Not a bit like those silly babies at school. And, oh, Mother, yesterday, he did forgive me, and I don't have to go out there any—any more!"

What a relief! It was all over. Dencey could go her own quiet way now—lead a respectable life and enjoy herself. She smiled through her tears.

Lydia bent solemnly and kissed her.

"Let us thank the Lord, Dionis," she said. "For it is He and not another that has put thee in this tender frame of mind."

Dencey squirmed a little, then knelt down by her mother's side. The very walls of "Mother's Room" must have known the feel of rising prayer.

As they got to their feet, Lydia said quietly:

"And now, Dionis, thee can go to the keeping room and mind little Hannah. Remember, Mother trusts thee that thee will never see Injun Jill's boy again."

How fatal the words sounded, not comfortable at all. Dencey's eyes clouded.

"But," she hesitated, "I have to give him back the book."

"What book?"

"*Pilgrim's Progress*. He gave it to me and ran back to Injun Jill so she couldn't hurt me. So—so I have to give it back."

"What does thee mean, child? Surely not the big *Pilgrim's Progress*? I have been looking everywhere for that to read to the little boys."

"But, Mother, it was my book. I gave it to Jetsam."

"Yes, Father gave it to thee. But it was really for all of us. We have no other copy. Where is it?"

"In my room."

"Go and get it."

Dencey went up to her room. Her feet were like lead upon the stair. She reached far under the bed and brought out the fat volume. It smote her with all the hours of labor she and Jetsam had spent upon it. The hiding in the sand, the escape of yesterday when Jetsam had thrust it into her hand. It was Jetsam's, that book, as preciously his as the house was Father's and Mother's.

She took it downstairs. Trembling, she gave it to her mother.

"It's Jetsam's," she said. "I gave it to him."

Lydia saw the book with horror.

"Why, it's ruined!" she exclaimed. "Thy beautiful

book from Father." She began turning over the dog-eared leaves.

"He couldn't help it," Dencey insisted. "Injun Jill tried to steal it from him, and he buried it in the Commons. It's Jetsam's," she repeated, a fear growing, growing in her heart. "I gave it to him."

"Thee did very wrong. It was not thine to give away."

"But I did give it to him. And he hasn't got any other. Please, Mother. We've got *Fox's Journal* and *Josephus* and *Besse's Sufferings*, and Jetsam's only got this. Don't take it away, Mother. Don't take it away!"

Dencey seemed to see Jetsam's dirty hand passing up and down over the cover.

Lydia sat silent in judgment. At last she said:

"Thee was wrong. But thee did give him the book, so the boy must have it. But does he care so much to read it?"

"Yes. Oh, yes. He works hard and gets every lesson. He reads almost as good as me."

Lydia smiled. "I'll tell thee what I'll do. I'll see the Fragment Society to-day and ask them to take him into their school, and I'll give the book to him myself."

"But I want to give it to him."

"Thee cannot. We agreed thee was not to see him again. He is not fit to play with thee or with any well-bred child."

Higher and higher came the rising tide of misery in Dencey's mind. Jetsam with the Fragment boys who hated him with united hatred. They'd never speak to him. They'd only stone him the way they always did. Jetsam was all alone now. How strange it would be when Mother gave him the book. Then he'd know Dencey despised him. Everybody despised him.

All the old pity and the burden of it came back, as if it fitted itself into a worn place on her shoulders. She couldn't despise Jetsam when everybody was despising him like that.

"Mother, I want to give him the book. Mother, I must give him the book." Dencey's voice was shrill. It sounded impudent.

"Dionis, what a strange turn! Thee must promise right now not to see the boy again."

An abyss had yawned. And Dencey stood on the brink of it. She answered never a word.

"Dionis, does thee hear me?"

"Yes, Mother," huskily. "But I won't promise."

"Dionis, what does thee mean? Thee said just now thee would never see him again."

"I—I didn't mean it. I won't promise." Her voice was loud again. It had a ring in it that Lydia should have recognized. For it was something of her own stubbornness— or shall one say, her martyr spirit?

"Dionis, I have to protect thee from slanderous tongues—things thee in no wise understands. Thee must never see the boy again, and thee has got to promise me that."

Dencey began to cry and sob. She was very frightened— as much at her own sudden determination as at her mother's gentle threats.

Lydia applied the last desperate remedies. Grandfather was to whip Dencey and then she was to stay in her own room on bread and water until she promised. The first was accomplished with much sorrow to all parties. Then Dencey was directed to her room. She looked at the white unbroken walls on which played the wavering reflection of the burnished sea.

"All the rest of my life I've got to sit here and see that," she thought.

For she knew she would never promise.

24. *The Unspeakable Jetsam*

THIS TIME LYDIA kept her promise. She went that same afternoon to the head of the Fragment Society and urged him to take Jetsam into the school. She explained how the boy already had mastered the art of reading with (Lydia hesitated) "almost no help at all."

"But," objected the old shipowner, "we have already tried that boy in the school. He failed—failed utterly. Bad as some of our poor boys are, that boy is worse. Lydia, thee must know that he is the worst boy in town. Lawless— perfectly lawless."

Lydia gasped but she kept her conscientious purpose. "Isn't that the more reason to reach out to him?" she asked. "Doesn't he need thy Fragment School more than thy other boys?"

"No, Lydia, no. He demoralizes the whole. We had him for a week. Why, the school was in turmoil. Fights in the yard the entire time. Boys coming in with broken heads. And at the end of that time the Jetsam boy ran away."

"Perhaps," Lydia said, remembering Dionis's earlier story—"perhaps the Fragment boys set upon him."

133

"Maybe they did. Maybe they did. If so, he was a match for all of 'em." The old man chuckled. "Anyways, Lydia"—he sobered—"when the teacher Keziah went for him she found him down by the wharf in the lowest pub. And when she bade him return, he blasphemed her. Oh, beyond all belief in so young a boy. Keziah's face burned telling it. No, no, Lydia. It's quite impossible to have him. I wonder at thee for urging it."

All this did not reassure Lydia as to her daughter's recent companion. How could her child, so well raised, have chosen him? And how could she have gone out to see him day after day? Horrible! Lydia walked home in a bad dream.

Yet she must deliver the *Pilgrim's Progress*. For so she had promised. She got old Ezra Coleman to take her in his cart out to Injun Jill's cabin—unspeakable place to be called home for anyone. But the boy was not there. Nor Injun Jill either. The house stood sagging and forlorn in the wide billows of the moors. Next day Lydia watched for the boy on State Street. She even ventured down to the wharf. All to no purpose.

Meanwhile, Dionis was still in her room. When Lydia went in, she was met by that obstinate, tragic little face. Three times a day Lydia put down the prison fare in front of her child, until the sight of the bread and water made Lydia sick. And all this was due to that ragamuffin of a boy whom the mother scarcely knew by sight.

"Child," said Lydia. "Remember, every time I come in, it is a chance for thee to speak. I am waiting for thy promise."

"I can't promise," Dencey returned. And later, with a stamp of her foot: "I won't promise."

There began in Lydia's mind a veritable hatred of the boy who had thus estranged her child. Had she been aware of the feeling, Lydia would have met and downed it. But she was too anxious over her problem with Dencey to notice this enemy of her spirit.

Not until Fourth Day morning did Lydia meet Jetsam on Orange Street.

"Wait," she commanded. "I have something for thee."

"What is it?" he returned. "A whuppin'?"

"Thee is an impudent boy," said Lydia, viewing with displeasure the smart grin on Jetsam's face. "No, I want to give thee thy book, *Pilgrim's Progress*. Wait where thee is. I will bring it."

She hurried home. She had no idea of bringing Jetsam to the gate and thus encouraging him about the place.

As she came back again, the pathos of the little waiting figure struck her in spite of her dislike. She actually thought of a rabbit on hind legs looking and listening. And when she gave him the book, how hungrily he snatched it.

"I thought she wus lyin'," he said, quite to the book—not to Lydia. Then he looked up. What wide-apart eyes conspicuous in his dirty face.

"Is it so that her granddad whups her every mornin' before breakfast?" he demanded.

"Whips? Does thee mean Dionis? Of course not!"

"The Coffin boys says so. They heard her scream. I reckon he does whup 'er."

His face whitened and began to quiver with fury. "He's got to stop it, the dirty scoundrel. She hain't done nothin'."

"I tell thee he does not whip Dencey," said Lydia angrily. But Jetsam had already darted down Stone Alley.

As Lydia went home, she suddenly realized that the ragged coat the boy had worn was the lost one of Stephen's. It seemed to effect a link between her daughter and the boy that baffled all her reasoning about it.

25. *The Prisoner*

MEANWHILE Dionis sat in her room.
The first day was not so bad. Dionis wept for two mortal hours which, after all, is an occupation in itself. Then she slept and did not waken until Mother brought in her bread-and-water supper. Then Mother and Steve took away Rosie's trundle bed. For Dencey must be quite alone. This was awful, of course. She was a criminal whom nobody must see or touch. Yet tragedy also is occupation.

The next day began the real trial of imprisonment—the minutes like hours, the hours like days. From her window she saw the fishing boats sail slowly out of the harbor into an infinity of iridescent pearl. She had always despised fishermen and their smelly nets. But, oh, how gladly would she have fished all her life—if only to get out and away.

The room was suffocating. She heard the boys talking downstairs. Companionship. She opened the door a crack to listen. Oh, dear, the pop-overs and coffee, how good they smelled. And just then Mother came in with bread and water.

Dencey turned her head from it.

"Take it away," she said wildly. "I won't eat it." And her mother silently departed.

There was no sense of guilt now—only the terrible sense of being trapped—some hidden thing that had snapped to and held her. She walked up and down the room—that room so filled with the live restlessness of the sea. The presence of the sea was at all the windows, but Dencey was held fast. She sat still in her chair looking out.

She could see Steve coming back from his work, and Kanah weeding the garden. She saw Peggy hang the clothes on the line. Such a lot. She counted them over and over. Hannah's dresses. And Ariel's cute little clothes, and, oh, a world of underthings for the four boys, and Jane's English muslin. That had been washed for sheep-shearing, for English goods was worn only on holidays.

The day seemed to ride like some grand Presence up over the arch of the sky; then, slowly, slowly decline down the changing west. And all the while the bells told off the hours of its life. The new Lisbon bell in the tower and the ships' bells in the harbor, each its own way—land language and sea language.

And each day as it came and passed over, moved more slowly than the last. A week had passed—two weeks. Dencey did not know. What difference did it make when she had to stay here always? She hardly ever thought of Jetsam or why she had to stay. She was too sorry for herself.

There began to grow in Dencey's mind a slow anger against her mother—Mother coming in three times a day with the horrid bread and water and saying the same thing. Lydia saw the anger growing and it terrified her. But what could she do? Lydia had been glad that Lovesta was away so that she could deal with her child unhampered. Now she wished with all her heart that Lovesta were here to help her out of the impasse.

Then came the worst day of all.

It had never occurred to Dencey that she could be left out of Sheep-shearing Day, that concentrated loveliness of all the days of the year. It was a compensation for Christmas, which the little Nantucketers never celebrated. But more adventurous than Christmas, out in the open Commons, under the open sky.

"But, Mother," wailed Dencey. "I have to go to Sheep-shearing. Nobody never doesn't go to the Shearing Day!"

"Yes, child, and Mother wants thee to go. There is no reason why thee shouldn't. Thee has only to promise."

"Promise," thought Dencey confusedly. Why, she'd almost forgotten all about it. Well, if she was shut up like this, she couldn't see Jetsam anyway. It was six of one and half a dozen of the other. Suppose she did promise. Then she could go to the Sheep-shearing. She looked up with that consent in her eyes which you see in a dog about to obey.

Lydia aided her a little.

"Thee knows thee doesn't have to play with Jetsam. Hopestill wouldn't dream of playing with him. Nor Elkanah, nor Bob. Why even the Fragment boys find him impossible. Captain Worth said so."

Ah, that was it. Nobody would play with Jetsam. Nobody would touch Jetsam—not even the Fragment boys. He was alone—alone. And how would it seem to turn her back on him if she met him on the street? She, Dencey Coffyn. How would he look when she did it? A frightened light flickered over Dencey's face.

"I can't promise," she said loudly. "I told thee I can't, and I can't."

Then, suddenly, she doubled up in her chair, like that little pine on the Commons, striving before a gale, and she wept and sobbed and gulped.

So Lydia left her.

26. *The Shearing*

S HEARING DAY DAWNED, tragic, beautiful as some impending Fate. It was full of the unearthly happenings that can take place only on Shearing Day.

The great baskets in the kitchen were piled high with hams, roast mutton, cake, gingerbread, and shearing-buns, and covered with Great-grandmother's napkins, woven especially for the Shearing Festival. Dencey knew this as she knew that the sun rose. She could hear the commotion in the kitchen—everybody busy making the morning tasks fly. Everybody in everybody else's way, but nobody mad about it, because it was Shearing Morning.

Ah, there came out Jane into the back yard taking in the big festive tablecloth that had been airing. A new wave of realization came over Dencey at the sight. For the awful truth seemed to forget itself at times and come over again in waves like that.

Oh, dear—oh, dear. Now she heard the clatter of the springless carts driving up to the front door, and the rush of the children through the hallway to pile into them.

They were going—all of them—actually going. Without her!

Suddenly Mother appeared, breathless and flushed with hurry. She put down a little basket.

"I thought it was right thee should have it," she said. "There's one of every kind"—she meant sandwiches— "and cake. And here's thy sampler."

Dencey was so angry that she dared not look up for fear it would burst out. She hid her face.

"Hopestill made the pound-rounds 'specially for thee," added Mother. She waited, but still Dencey did not speak. Then Mother went away.

And now the two carts went clattering down the cobbled street.

A deathly silence fell upon the house which had been so full of glad, living clamor. The voice of the sea gradually became audible in the room, whispering over and over as if it would say something but never saying it. The wind sighed about the corners of the house and shook the shutters. Dencey's misery settled down over her like a cloud.

She didn't cry out loud, only the tears seemed like a teacup that was too full and kept joggling over. And Mother thought sandwiches and cake could make up for losing the Shearing Festival. If she threw the basket out of the window, then Mother'd see how she felt.

Ah, there went another cart clattering down the street. That would be the Severances, and Hopestill in among them. Another cart still. The Joys would be in that. Yet another cart went by, and after a silent interval, two more.

Suddenly, it occurred to Dencey that she was the only one left on North Water Street. Everybody had gone to the Shearing. Why, for the matter of that, she was the

only one in the whole town. In all Nantucket were just
empty houses, and she sitting alone in the emptiest one
of all. In spite of the bright sunshine, Dencey began to be
afraid. She cowered down in her chair by the open window. Out there by the harbor were the docks. Fiji men
were at the docks working. They wouldn't go to the Shearing. Stephen had told her long ago that Fijis were canni-
bals. That meant they ate folks instead of mutton, and
they especially liked little girls with black hair.

She knew Stephen had been pretending. But maybe he
was only pretending to pretend. Maybe it was all so.
Dencey thought she heard steps coming up the stair—
up—up—up. They came to the door, paused, and went
down again. It was only the wind.

In desperation she took up her sampler and began to
stitch as hard as ever she could. But she wasn't seeing the
roses or the little willow trees she was stitching. She was
seeing—all the while, seeing the Commons way out there
by Miacomet Pond and folks arriving from all the roads
there were. Carefree faces under the solemn Quaker bonnets, laughing faces under the Quaker hats. And the Congregationalists too, for all Nantucket came to the Shearing Festival; and even people from the Cape and the Main.

Oh, Mother didn't know how much Dencey wanted to
be there! Nobody could possibly know.

Now all the sheep would be in the pen—everybody's
sheep from the whole Island. White as fleecy clouds, they
crowded into the place. For yesterday they had all been
washed in the pond. How fresh the wind blew out there,
so far from everywhere. How the booming surf sounded all
through the laughing, chattering voices, for the outer shore
was just beyond the pond. So Dencey had heard it every

year since before memory began. How blue, blue was the pond, how white the sheep, how intensely green the Commons. Dencey always saw things in color.

By now the men would be coming with the shears. The poor sheep didn't like it. Look how the sheep oil dripped from the long clipping scissors and even from the elbows of the shearers. Well, anyway, the sheep ought to be glad not to be smothered in that heavy greasy wool. How fast the men worked and marked up on the fence rail the number of sheep they had sheared. When the fence rail was full of marks, and all the naked sheep had scampered away on the grass, then everybody would have dinner.

What was that?

Dionis was aware of a whistle. She was aware that it had been whistling again and again, only she hadn't heard it. The Fijis were come! They were whistling to each other. The Fijis! Down there in the back yard!

In a fascination of terror she crept to the window. She peeped down into the yard. What was it down there? Fijis were naked. The person down there had clothes on. The person down there wasn't a man but a boy. Oh, it was Jetsam!

"Hi, there," he called, delighted. "Wus ye asleep? I thought ye wus dead."

A flourish of joy swept through Dencey, a fanfare. Relief, safety, companionship, adventure! All suddenly out of the blue.

"Well, can't ye say nothin'?" complained Jetsam. "Cat got yer tongue?"

"How did thee get here?" she called down rapturously.

"On my two feet."

"But thee isn't at the Shearing."

"I don't keer fur the ole Shearin'."

This was a lie and Dencey knew it. But what a glorious lie! Dencey hung recklessly out of the window.

"They'll be eating dinner right now. Thee won't get thine." For even Jetsam got a royal dinner on Shearing Day.

"I don't keer. They was all thar. Yer ma an' Peg Runnel an' all. I counted 'em. So I knew ye wus here by yerself. Say, do they whup ye every day or only every other?"

"They don't whip me at all," declared Dencey, offended.

"Don't? Honest Injun?" Jetsam was unbelieving.

"Yes, Honest Injun Jill!"

At this sally of wit they laughed uproariously.

Jetsam came right under the window.

"Say," he called secretly, "come down."

Dencey's heart thumped with amazement. Of course she couldn't do that.

"Nobody's goin' to see us. We kin go 'way out yander by the cliff. Nobody's in the hull town."

"I can't."

"Oh, yes, ye kin. Come along. Look what I got."

He held up a neat package in a beautiful napkin—sand-wiches done up in the conventional manner.

"We kin go anywhar ye want. I'll take ye down to the docks. Ye know they won't be home till sundown."

Wonderful, wonderful.

"Say, why don't ye answer?"

She didn't answer because she was thinking too hard. There was her own basket of lunch also. Why, they could have a feast. Almost as good as the Shearing. Better than the Shearing!

"Wait," she called.

She did not stop for her bonnet. She picked up the

basket and dashed down the stairway, then the lower stairway to the kitchen.

There, in the great, empty, familiar kitchen, something arrested her. What was it? The room so neatly arranged in spite of this morning's haste, the pans bright upon the mantelshelf, the fire carefully covered for the return, and the kettle on its crane. Her own dress and kerchief hung up, meticulously ironed by Mother in the hope that she would promise and be allowed to go.

If Dencey left this now, she would never see it again. She was sure of it. Her love of it was as instinctive as breathing, as strong as the muscles of her body.

And, moreover, Jetsam's lunch was stolen!

Without a moment's hesitation, she turned and ran upstairs again. She appeared at the window.

"What the deuce!" called Jetsam.

"I'm not going."

Jetsam swore a series of oaths all fastened together.

"Thee stop that," called Dencey through her tears. "I can't go, no matter what thee says."

"Would they whup ye so bad?"

She nodded.

Somehow that satisfied Jetsam. Whippings for himself were in the course of nature. But Dencey was a different matter.

"Say," he said, "I'll give ye this hyar lunch. I'll put it on the kitchen steps fur ye."

"I couldn't eat that," declared Dencey, "because thee stole it."

"I didn't."

"Oh, yes, thee did, Sam Jetsam."

"Well, anyway, they'll not miss it. They had heaps an'

piles."

"Thee take it back and I'll give thee half of mine. It's got jelly cake."

The cake or some dawning repentance at last persuaded Jetsam. Then Dencey procured a rope from the boys' room, took out half the lunch for herself and let down the other half in the basket to Jetsam.

What fun! What infinite fun after the long tiresome do-nothing days!

"Oh, Jetsam," she called. "I'll give thee another sermon to read."

"I hain't finished that un yet," he answered. "Writin's the very mischief."

"I'll find a plainer one. Thee wait."

She drew the basket up.

In Dencey's room a ladder led up to a trapdoor where was the garret. It was a small trapdoor, and Dencey could lift it. This she proceeded to do. Up in the garret she overturned a barrel of her uncle's sermons, searched hastily till she found a plainly written one. It concerned the death of George the Third and began with the terrific sentence, "George, George, George is no more!"

She hurried down again, and lowered the sermon in the basket. Halfway down it fluttered out and Jetsam had to chase the leaves hither and yon. George was "no more" all over the yard.

Suddenly, before he had secured a half of the pages, came the sound of old Mrs. Joy's voice next door.

"Sam Jetsam, how dares thee come in that yard! I'll tell Mrs. Coffyn, that I will."

And Jetsam flew with that swiftness known only to the bad boy.

27. Pure Magic

DIONIS WAS ALONE again. No, not alone. Evidently Mrs. Joy had been detailed to watch her from next door. Dencey ate her lunch and still had the whole afternoon before her, blank and eventless.

Suddenly she noticed the ladder and the open trap-door.

Then came the most wonderful event of the day.

Dencey climbed up the ladder. To go downstairs seemed very wicked, but it was perfectly proper to go up. There, in the glimmering garret, were the dresses hanging in a row from the rafters, and on top of some, bonnets that looked as though they would nod. There were the coco shells scattered on the floor that the boys had got from a wreck. She had seen these hundreds of times. And there was the overturned barrel. For very boredom, she began to search among the sermons, taking them out to the very bottom, all unaware of the wonder that lay just beyond her finger tips.

Who can disbelieve in the ringing of fairy bells, mysterious trysts, "angels and ministers of grace," when such things as this can happen:

Dencey's hand came upon something hard. She drew out a little sheep-bound book like a hymn book. She opened it in the middle—a gobbling way she had—*The Arabian Nights Entertainments!*

A little copper-plate picture of an enchanted horse and a princess with trousers on. That was all.

She was aware of nothing more.

The walls of the garret grew far and lordly, then melted in an incoming flood of Oriental sunshine. Jewels flashed, terrible blood-curdling murders were toward, people stepped on ordinary-looking carpets and were whisked at once into the air. A fairy lived in a well and came out to quarrel over who was the most beautiful prince in the world. Time was not, for pure joy is timeless.

Then, blindingly, the world fell.

"Dionis, what is thee doing? How dared thee leave thy room?"

There was Mother standing halfway out of the trap-door like a ghost out of a grave.

"I thought at least thee was honorable enough to stay in thy room. And why did thee throw papers all over the yard?"

Still Dencey did not answer. It was not easy to come all the way from Bagdad to Nantucket.

"Dionis, what is thee reading?"

Dazedly, Dencey handed her the book. Mother looked at it with darkening brow.

"Come down," she said sternly. And Dencey followed her down the ladder.

"Dionis, why does thee seem to find evil as though thee were its magnet? This is a book which belonged to Father. Grandfather told me to burn it. But I hid it at the bottom of a barrel. Oh, dear, I see how wrong I was!"

"Mother," cried out Dencey, aghast, "thee wouldn't burn it."

"I certainly will. Grandfather says it is a worldly, wicked book."

"It isn't. It isn't. It's the beautifullest book in the whole world. Thee sha'n't do it."

Mother started toward the door. Dionis flashed after her and snatched the book from her hand. An unseemly struggle ensued. Lydia had all she could do to get the book back again. When she did get it, Dencey's smouldering anger burst all bounds. She stamped her foot, gasping out strange words she didn't know herself.

"Thee is mean—mean and wicked. Thee is a wicked and slothful servant. Thee is—thee is——"

Mother caught her shoulder. And the look on Mother's face silenced all words.

"Dionis, the book has evidently done its worst with thee. Oh, must I have Grandfather whip thee all over again?"

Again Dionis sat waiting in her room. Oh, would she always be waiting there for something dreadful to happen! Now Grandfather would be coming up to whip her. She couldn't stand it to be whipped now. It wasn't like the first time. She was afraid.

More afraid than she was of the Fijis. Grandfather's legs weren't good but his arm was terribly strong. He used to whip sailors on shipboard once, when he was mate.

Oh, there was his step on the stair. Her heart thumped one awful thump and kept on thumping. The lower stair, the upper stair, he was coming so fast.

The door opened.

There appeared, not Grandfather, but Aunt Lovesta. Aunt Lovesta back from her far journey. Aunt Lovesta, smiling. With a cry, Dencey rushed to her, clasped arms about the strong waist, burying her face against the soft warm kerchief, and getting it all wet with her tears.

Then, somehow, she was sitting on a little stool with her head in Aunt Lovesta's lap. Aunt Lovesta was stroking her hair and with every stroke comfort was flowing over and over. She was telling Aunt Lovesta everything. And Aunt Lovesta was telling her back, making everything clear.

It appeared that some of the worst things weren't wicked at all, and some other things were very wrong. It appeared that she could divide the promise up. Not promise it all in one gulp. She could be kind to Jetsam when she saw him. She could give him food and clothes and books. She could bring him to see Aunt Lovesta. But she must not go out on the Commons to meet him. And she must promise that and faithfully keep it.

"But does thee like the boy so much, Dionis? Does thee like him as thee does Hopestill?" asked Aunt Lovesta.

"Why, o' course not," said Dencey, open-eyed. "Hopestill's my very most intimate friend."

"Thee is sure thee'd rather not be with the Jetsam boy than with Hopestill or any other companions?"

Dencey blushed indignantly.

"Why, Aunt Lovesta, thee doesn't suppose I'd be silly about a boy like Jane or Peggy!"

And Aunt Lovesta smiled merrily.

28. *Jetsam in the Lane*

THERE FOLLOWED a calm summer. Dionis was well content to be at home in the protected ways she had so strangely lost. Lydia began to think that the punishment seemingly so disastrous had been good after all. And Lovesta said:

"Yea, Lydia, the Light lieth in her as a naked seed in stony ground, but it is there."

Dionis often saw Jetsam, saw him when on her errands or when he passed the house, which it must be acknowledged he often did. Dencey conducted him, after much persuasion, to Aunt Lovesta's, where he stood like a bird you have caught and hold between your two hands, perfectly still, watching with bright eyes. Aunt Lovesta could get nothing out of him.

"Dencey, child," she said afterward, "doubtless thee sees something in the boy. But I'm afraid he is rather dull and ill-born."

"I don't know about his being ill-born. But he isn't dull, Aunt Lovesta. He learned to read as quick, as quick."

Far away on the Mainland the summer grew and sizzled. Nobody minded. Nobody dreamed of going away to avoid it. As for Nantucket, one beautiful day followed another—cool, breathful, fragrant—the gift of the sea.

Hopestill and Dencey ran together as two streams that had been parted by some temporary dam. Indeed, there were four girls who were inseparable. They were too old for dolls, but they had staid tea parties in each other's yards. They went to the quiltings and were newly allowed to sit at the busy gossipy frame and sew the fine, fine stitches into an almost invisible pattern. Once, at a tea party in Dencey's yard, Jetsam came and stood outside watching. Dencey could see his eyes peering between the palings of the fence. She was ashamed. Already Susan and Kate and Hopestill were pretending she had a beau. It was a great joke, for, of course, the Jetsam boy wasn't a fit beau for anybody. Sedulously, Dencey turned her back on Jetsam.

Sometime later, Dencey, with a crowd of youngsters, was careering up State Street toward the Madeket Road. They all had pails and were bound for blueberries.

Jetsam appeared out of a lane, and one of the boys remarked:

"There's Injun Jill's boy—the one Dencey Coffyn got locked up for. Hey, Dence, why don't thee go with him instead of us?"

Dencey blushed crimson and tossed her head. Then, as they turned a corner, she glanced back.

Yes, there he was, Jetsam. His eyes looked as if he had lost something. He was all alone, as usual—the one pariah.

With a mighty effort, Dencey turned.

"I'll be right back," she called, as she ran toward him.

"Sam Jetsam," she said angrily. "What makes thee pop out of a lane and stare at me like that? Thee's got to stop it."

For a wonder, Jetsam was not angry in return. He only said gloomily:

"Yes, ye're ashamed of me. Everybody's ashamed of me, and you, too."

"No, I'm not. At least, I was a little bit when the boys taunted me."

Jetsam did look miserable.

"But I won't be any more," said Dencey.

"It isn't won't be," he answered. "Ye jist are."

At that moment, who should turn into State Street but Liakim Cole, the Clerk of the Meeting—gaunt, dignified, absorbed in mighty matters, clicking his cane as he went along. In a community where none were supposed to be lordly the Clerk was lordliest of all. It was he took the *sense* of the meeting without vote and reported to the higher powers.

Dencey moved close to Jetsam's side, her shoulder touching.

"How does thee do, Friend Liakim," she sang out. Right to the Clerk of the Meeting. Boldness could no farther go.

The mighty one stopped—beetled his brow at the two standing there. It so happened that at that moment the old man had been mortal lonely.

"How does thee do, child," he answered. "What a bright voice. Is thee and thy friend going berrying?"

"Jetsam and me are friends," shouted Dencey.

"So I see," said the old man, puzzled, and went on clicking his cane down the street.

"There," announced Dencey. "I stood with thee right before the Clerk. That shows I'm not ashamed."

Then, without waiting for answer, she dashed off to catch up with her crowd.

29. *Sparks That Fly Upward*

LYDIA COFFIN WAS having a veal feast. That meant that early in the morning Homer Cobb had come and killed the calf—a performance witnessed, I am sorry to say, by all the boys and even Jane. The meat had been cut up and was now ready for distribution. Grandfather Coffyn would have his share at home with the family tomorrow. Meanwhile, the portions must be carried to old Uncle Sylvanus Coffin and Cousin Scottow Coffin, etc., etc., for, in a veal feast, the relatives on the male side were served first. Then came Lydia's three sisters and her brother Caleb just home from a voyage. Each portion had been placed on a large plate and covered with veal-feast napkins woven specially for the purpose. It was a busy day.

Dencey and Kanah had the joyous duty of carrying the plates to the relatives. It meant pleasant welcomes, and compliments (paid to the veal, of course, as personal compliments were excess of vanity). And then sweet rounds stuffed into a child's pocket as she went away.

Now Dencey was starting out with the last plate, for Aunt Mehitable Severance, who lived at the other end of the town.

Summer was gone. Autumn was come. From some hidden treasuries of the sky, wine rubies and fire were poured down upon the Commons. The distances shouted with scarlet. The sea-girt solitude celebrated some mystic festival of its own beyond human power to enter. When Dionis had driven across the moorland with Aunt Lovesta, she astonished that relative by speaking not one word the whole way. But now that theophany was over and its place of divine showing gone gray, for it was late November.

The day was one of those chance gifts of an austere season, warm and slumberous, with a haze over the sea. As Dencey glanced out over the harbor, all the sloops and fishing boats seemed in a dream, "thinking delicate thoughts." Strange that on such a beautiful morning all the boats should be huddling into the harbor instead of going on their widespread errands.

Speaking of errands, Dencey must not loiter upon hers. So she hurried along with her plate toward State Street. Dencey had been "good" for a long time. She had no wish to be otherwise now, as she stopped so innocently to read a poster tacked up on the Rotch Warehouse.

What a poster it was! It bore a picture, a man balancing a staff upon his chin in a purely miraculous manner, and on the top of the staff was a doll, or perhaps a living child. Dionis feasted upon this woodcut for a whole minute before reading the text. (Alas, well has the Good Book said, "Born to trouble as sparks that fly upward.")

Professor Sylvanus Snubshoe
On Tuesday Eve. Nov 28, 1822
Will display the Nesico's Box
Rope-dancing, wire-walking and 100 deceptions
To wh. will be added
An imitation of a Bagpipe and A British Officer.
The whole to conclude with the surprising powers of
the Ventriloquist
He possesses by nature the power of causing a voice to
be heard in all parts of the room and Closits
He causes the voice of a child to be heard in a
Tea Pot!
and exclaim "Let me out, Let me out, or I shall
smother!"
The same voice will be heard in any
Gentleman's snuff-box or Ladie's Thimble.
Mr Snubshoe will throw his voice into a Cod Fish
which will immediately make a noise like that of a Hog.
He will cause an Oyster to imitate a number of Birds
To give a minute detail of this exhibition would fill
volumes
Admission 50¢. Children a shilling
Doors open at 6 o'clock
Performance at 7
Washington Hall

Dionis read it to its glowing end. She probably did not
breathe while reading it, for, at the final word, "Children
a shilling," her breath came back in a long shuddering
gasp. Then the Wish sprang into being.

If that Wish could have been seen, how it would have

towered above her—a bright shape "pulling her backward by the hair."

Oh, if she could attend that performance. "Doors open at six o'clock." These wonders actually on Nantucket Island—not in some far-off port of Peru or the Antarctic, but here at home, to be touched and handled by the commoner, beheld by the public eye.

And she had a shilling. Uncle Caleb had given her a shilling when he came home. She had supposed she would keep it until she was grown up. But what was the use of growing up if thee missed a marvel like this—a chance never to be repeated in a lifetime.

The manner of going did not occur to her, the sin of it was afar off. There was only the Wish.

Suddenly a voice at her elbow.

"What ye doin' hyar—starin' with yer mouth wide open?"

It was Jetsam. He had a way of appearing from nowhere like that.

Dencey shut her mouth and swallowed.

"Oh, I wish I could see that," she said. "I wish—" Her voice trailed off for very intensity.

"See what?" he asked.

"Why, what the poster says. He can make a codfish grunt like a hog. And an oyster talk—no, sing. 'Sing like a number of birds.'" She corroborated it in actual reading.

"Aw, he can't. An oyster—whew!"

"Yes, he can. Look at the reading and the pictures."

Jetsam began to read the poster. Many words were troublesome, as "Professor" and "Nesico." Dencey grew impatient. She began to read it to him in clear inspired tones. Jetsam took fire at them.

"Lordy!" he exclaimed. "By Crick, makes his voice come out of a closet, does he?"

"And out of a teapot," emphasized Dencey.

"I'm goin'," announced Jetsam, without finishing the poster. "I'm goin' to-night."

"To-night," repeated Dencey faintly. Brought down thus to reality, it gave her a shock.

"I'm afraid it's wicked," she ventured. "Thee—thee ought not to go."

"Ye'd go if ye dast, but ye don't dass."

Dencey, the honest, knew this to be so.

"Hit's no more wicked to hold a cane on yer chin than in yer hand. Hit's jist tricks."

"I couldn't go to Washington Hall," said Dencey.

"Yes, ye could. I'd wait fer ye at the door and slip ye in so nobody ud see ye. It'll be after dark."

"After dark!"

"Yes, silly. That don't hurt. Put on somebody's oiler an' sou'wester an' nobody'll know ye."

Dencey's eyes sparkled. Disguise, night, flight, and the wonders of magic!

"I'll come," she said. "Thee be sure to be there—at the door."

"Of course I will." Sam put his arms akimbo. "An' I won't let no dirty rascal hurt ye neither," he said.

30. *The Horrible Professor Snubshoe*

SUDDENLY BOTH OF them felt a presence. Sam saw it first and flashed around the corner like a swallow. Dencey faced around. It was none other than Aunt Susanna Severance, a relative more feared than loved by the youngsters. She belonged to what Peggy Runnel called the "Squelchin' Committee" and that office seemed never absent from her thoughts.

"Why, Dencey Coffyn," she commented. "I do wonder at thee, loitering when thee has a veal plate to carry. Doesn't thee suppose somebody's waiting for it? What was thee doing?"

Then her eye fell on the poster.

"Dionis Coffyn, I'm not surprised thee is a subject of uneasiness to thy mother. Reading about a stage play. Of all things!"

She leaned forward, pushing back her bonnet and pouncing on the poster. Dencey couldn't help noticing that, even for Aunt Susanna, it had interest. She read it through to the end.

"Horrible! Horrible!" she pronounced. "Right here on the Island in Washington Hall. I don't see how they dare."

Dionis longed to run but was too polite.

"I shall ask Liakim Cole if it can't be torn down. A stage play in Nantucket!"

Just at this moment a diversion was created. There came out of the "Captain's Room" of the Warehouse a man—such a man! His hair was longish and oily so it stained the shoulders of his coat. His moustache was elaborate. He was big and burly, yet suave—too suave. He was a Yankee, which made it all the worse.

The nice fresh-flowered soul of the little girl recoiled from him, strangely knowing the evil in him.

"Admirin' my poster, air ye," he said boldly to Aunt Susanna. "Well, it's a good un, ef I do say it. And the best on't 'tis—it's true. I kin do it all. Every darn bit of it, jest as it's writ down."

He could do it! Dencey's magic heaven came clattering about her ears. Was he, then, the magician—this common, horrible man?

But he was rattling on very fast.

"The fust time ye see my show, ma'am, wun't be the last. Ye'll come agin and—"

"I!" interrupted Aunt Susanna's deep organ voice. "I see thy stage play? Never! I value my immortal soul too dear. I am reading thy notice that I may report it to the Committee on Sufferings and have it torn down. I'll gladly tear it down with my own hand."

The man laughed rudely.

"Shocks ye, does it?"

Imagine this to Aunt Susanna—Clerk of the Woman's Meeting—"Well, good enough. I'm glad to shock ye kill-joy Quakers, ennaway. Ef suthin' cud jist shock ye enough to make ye give yer dead some gravestuns instid o' shovin' 'em in the ground like they was cats an' dogs, an' git yer young folks married decent with a preacher—"

All this, and the lightning did not strike him nor the sky fall upon him!

However, Aunt Susanna did.

"How dares thee!" she cried. "How dares thee blaspheme God's elect and the ways taught by the Seed of Truth! Thy notice shall surely come down and thy wicked performings be forbidden in the Island."

"Ye won't, nuther, ye—ye—ye—" The man stepped threateningly toward Aunt Susanna, swearing some oath.

Just then the spell of horror which had held Dencey broke, and she fled.

Up State Street, on and on, carrying her plate of veal carefully amid a surrounding tumult of thoughts. Friends—Quaker Friends to be evilly spoken of, their sacred ways questioned, and that by an Off-Islander! Why, he wasn't even born on Nantucket, much less belonged to one of the "families." That horrid, horrid man!

Gradually other thoughts came back.

She had been going to that stage play—planned it with Jetsam. The fiery pit had yawned. Only Aunt Susanna had snatched her back—a brand from the burning. But Jetsam—he would go. He would wait there for her at the door of that dread place.

She almost dropped her plate, saved it by a miracle, and hurried up to Aunt Mitty's door.

Aunt Mitty was puzzled by her.

"Can't thee tell me any news to-day? Why is thee in such a hurry? Here's a cup full of pickled limes for thee.

Thee can eat two on the way home, but the rest is for Mother. Thee must bring back the cup. Dencey—does thee hear—"

But Dencey was already down the path again. There, in the road, a blessed assurance came to her. Aunt Susanna said the show must be broken up. And what Aunt Susanna said was surely performed. Perhaps, by this time, the man was even aboard a vessel sailing out of the harbor—he and all his wicked magic. Then Jetsam would be safe.

The magnificent wish to go to the show had died at one blow at the appearance of the showman—the cruel, snake-like, commonplace showman. She wouldn't want to see anything that man could do. The very thought of him gave her "the creeps."

Aunt Susanna was terrible as an accuser but now, as a deliverer, she was a tower of strength. Yet, even so, Dencey looked up and down the street hoping to see Jetsam and warn him. Passing the Rotch Warehouse she gave one fearful glance. Ah, the poster was gone. Susanna Victrix!

Dencey went home comforted. All that day a calm of deliverance was upon her.

Next day, toward noon, Mother sent her out to put Nelly-cow in the shed because the wind had gone around north. As Dencey shut the shed door, she heard a familiar whistle, and there was Jetsam, very indignant.

"Why didn't ye come, ye 'fraid-cat. I waited fer ye till half-past seven."

"Waited? Where?" A wild startle shook Dencey's mind.

"Why, at Washington Hall, goosey. But the show wasn't thar. It was moved to Waco's Sail Loft, next to Dicky Dicks's pub. I was goin' to take ye."

"But, Jetsam," queried Dencey's scared voice, "there

wasn't any show. Aunt Susanna—"

"Aunt Susanna nothin'! O' course she kicked at it. But he only moved it down to the dock streets. An', oh, Crick, it was grand. He made the babby yell out o' the teapot like the paper said. I wus so sorry fer it, I was pushin' through the crowd to git it out my own self when, all of a twink, hit was in the back o' the room. Yellin'—'I'm out. I'm out.' An' ye couldn't see it—not a thing."

Dencey opened the back gate and came out. She wanted to be nearer Jetsam.

"Oh, Jetsam, did thee go to that wicked show?"

"O' course I went to it." Jetsam was nonplussed. "Didn't ye tell me about it? Didn't ye plan to go, too?"

"Yes—yes—I did." Dionis kept clasping and unclasping her hands.

Jetsam regarded her with scorn.

"Sissy! I didn't think ye'd be so afeard of yer Aunt Susanna."

"It wasn't her. It was that man—the showman. He was so horrid and oily and he said swears."

"But he didn't swear in the show," persisted Jetsam.

"Oh, it wasn't the swears. It was *him*," declared Dencey. She was puzzled trying to express what she knew so certainly. "He—he was bad. He was so hairy. Oh, Jetsam, how could thee watch him doing anything? I'd as leave watch a snake or—or an octopus."

"He wasn't wicked, I tell ye. He was funny. He made me laugh till I got a stitch in my side. He made everybody laugh."

"Oh, Jetsam, don't think it was funny. Think of thy soul. People that go to vain shows and pastimes, they go—to—hell."

She paused before the sepulchral word.

Jetsam jeered angrily. Truth to tell, he was disappointed. He had expected to boast about the show. And here Dencey was talking about his soul! He had something else to tell, too.

"I'm goin' with him!" he announced.

She merely stared in speechless unbelief. "Yes, I'm goin' with him—off-island—to the Continent. Mebbe to Boston. I'm goin' to help him with the show. He's hired me—for wages!"

Sam stood with legs apart to watch the effect. It was all that could be desired. Dencey seized his shoulders and shook him.

"Thee isn't, thee isn't, Sam Jetsam. Thee wouldn't go with that man. Oh, Sam, isn't thee just teasing?"

Indeed, he was teasing, and enjoying it hugely. Dencey had neglected him of late. Now, here she was shaking his shoulders, pleading with him. Why, she was crying. He laughed straight out. Besides, it was true—this news. The man had said he would take Jetsam. Only the wage part was a lie.

"Hi, ye're mad," Jetsam said. "Ye wanted to go just onct, and I'm goin' every night, yes—'ceptin' when we're on shipboard or lookin' at Boston."

Dencey became more quiet as the awful truth became plain.

"Sam, I'll give thee that other book, I'll find it again in the attic. It's ten times nicer than *Pilgrim*. It's about geniis and princes and fairies. I'll give thee my fan coral, I'll give thee—"

But at all of these Sam shook and reshook his head.

"I'm *goin'*," he said. "To-morrow mornin' on the packet.

The man hired me."

All of a sudden, he wrenched himself free from her grasp and fled.

Dencey stood there, her teeth chattering in the cold wind. Her mind racing with witch thoughts and terrors.

"Dencey, Dencey!" Her mother's voice at last penetrated her mind. "I've been calling thee for ten minutes and thee right there. Take the pail and go to the street pump for me."

31. *Dencey Makes Up Her Mind*

DENCEY GAVE HER mother the dripping pail and then climbed upstairs to her own room. The calamity was so great that it stilled her mind like a smoothed-out sea before a storm.

Jetsam was lost—utterly lost. All the horrors of hell, its fleshly burning and inward soul agony which her grandfather had so aptly described, came back to her. It was to this that Jetsam was descending. And *Pilgrim's Progress* told all about it. And Jetsam would be there forever and forever, he and that terrible man.

Mother called her to wash the raisins for plum broth. The veal feast made a busy day of cooking. Dencey went obediently downstairs and sat hour long at the task, thinking, thinking.

She had done this deed. She alone. If she had not stopped in front of the notice and asked Jetsam to read it, he would never have known about the show. Oh, dear, oh, dear, and she begged him to go, she had planned to go with him. It was all her doing. His sin was on her soul.

And now Jetsam was going away with the showman. The showman would be cruel to him. And Jetsam was going to hell forever and forever.

"Dence Coffyn," said Peggy, shaking her, "can't thee answer a civil question? Thee can usually talk mor'n enough. And thee's washed twice too many raisins. Why, of all things!"

Then Dencey went upstairs again.

Only gradually did the dread thoughts retire enough to let a plan of action come in.

If she could find Jetsam, and tie him to a post or something. Where could she find a rope? Where could she find Jetsam? Down there among the docks and the ships and the sailors. Oh, she didn't know where he was! And to-morrow morning he would go.

She stole down to her grandfather's room to look at the tide table. Yes, tide would be high at 3 A.M. The packet would weigh anchor then to catch the flood tide. Three A.M. The dead of night. And that man with him. That wicked man!

Young as she was, Dencey actually wrung her hands. But she was silent—silent. The purposes forming in her brain kept her so. Purpose after purpose made and rejected.

The rope was foolish, of course. Could she give him anything? No, she had offered him every treasure. But, if she could find him, she could keep him back. She would clutch him with both hands and drag him up the street to Mother. Mother wouldn't let him go to hell.

She crept downstairs to find Mother. It was in her heart to tell Mother everything. But Lydia was not there. Little Ariel was sick and she had taken him to the doctor.

Dencey looked out the window. The pale November sunshine had given place to gray cloud. A snow fell half-heartedly and swirled like white dust along the streets. There was no time to lose. She must go quickly now, before dark. She must save Jetsam.

She went to her mother's room. Found some paper on which she wrote a note, which she pinned on Mother's pincushion, then down to the back hall, where she put on her pleater and warmest cloak.

Then out at the front door.

Whew, how the wind caught her! And the snow pricked her cheeks like little pins.

She stood, clutching her cloak, wondering where to go. Then, suddenly, she recalled Dicky Dicks's boarding house down by the water's edge. Jetsam had often spoken of it. For Dicky sometimes let him sleep in the taproom on stormy nights. The place was the peculiar care of the sheriff for its midnight fights and worse. But Dencey did not know that. She started at once. It was just the sort of weather for Jetsam to be there.

The pleasant home streets were left behind. She was threading her way in the twisted lanes crowded with water life. Here bales and hogsheads, there anchors tumbled in front of ship-hardware shops, and everywhere drays unloading at the doors—the men blocking the path with their burdens.

Oh, the forbidden streets again. A wicked sin to come here! But Dencey brushed the thought aside as one would brush away a fly. Jetsam's danger overwhelmed all else.

The first man she asked the way was a Portuguese who stared and grinned at her, not understanding a word of English. The next was a true Yankee.

"Ye hain't no business at that pub, miss," he said.

"It isn't business," said Dionis breathlessly, blinking her eyelashes with snow. "He's—he's there, and I've got to find him and take him home."

"Gol darn the ole drunk," commented the Yankee. He pointed her the way to the boarding house. "Now, ef yer pap ain't thar, ye come right out," he advised. "He hain't no right to bring ye thar."

Dionis stood fearfully by the closed door of Dicky Dicks's. There is no telling when she would have found courage to enter; but a noisy crew of sailors suddenly bore down upon the place, and Dencey was hurried in, in their wake.

A dreadful-looking man was Dicks, the barkeep. At first, Dionis could not bring herself to speak to him. A gash ran up one cheek ending in his eye—ending the eye, in fact, for there was none there. The thing stabbed Dencey with actual pain. And the man himself, jolly as a cricket, running hither and yon to serve the sailors with grog.

But at last Dionis got his attention.

"Jetsam? Injun Jill's Jetsam? Ye want him?" he asked. "Air ye the little gal he talks about?"

"Is he here?" she insisted. "Oh, I must see him quick."

"Well, no, he hain't. I'm sorry. He was here the forepart o' the afternoon helping the showman he's a-goin' with. Had to work, I tell ye. But now he's went out to the cabin to split some last kindlin' fer Injun Jill."

"Oh," pleaded Dionis, "if he comes back here, don't let him go with that man—please."

"Well, now," said Dick, plunging a red-hot poker into a jug of ale, "I wisht I could keep 'im back. But ye can't do nuthin' with Jetsam. That man Snubshoe was jailed in

New Bedford fer some bad doin's o' his. Jetsam's a fool to go with him, ef ye ask me."

But Dionis wasn't "asking" him. Hadn't she known all that from the beginning?

"Don't let Jetsam go with him," she said again.

Then she ran out the door.

The little street was already attired in white—all suddenly clean and silent. The roofs seemed to cosey down beneath the snow as if some kindliness were touching them. The gables, set this way and that, shouldering forward on the crooked lane, nodded solemnly to each other.

"Dencey's going out to the Commons again," they seemed to be telling. "She's going out to meet Jetsam on the Commons, and she promised she wouldn't."

A sob suddenly caught Dencey's throat.

"Oh, Aunt Lovesta," she said aloud. "I'm sorry I broke my promise to thee."

She spoke as though it were already done, so certain was she of doing it. All up the street the word followed her mind. "My promise—my promise." All up the street and to the Mill Road.

"I didn't mean to do it, Auntie," she said again.

The mills on the hill were astonished and lifted up their snowy arms against her. Not one mill sail was moving. They were all stripped and locked against the storm.

In the town the snow had come down dreamily but out here on the Commons it was hurried by the wind, driven in clouds and gusts. It wasn't like snow but like a fine white mist. Everywhere the wind moaned. It seemed to be talking in her ears. She could hear the sea crashing against the distant beaches.

Out here on the Island was a big white world.

Dionis looked back. Already the town was hidden, and even the mills looked dim in the curtains of snow.

"It's a good thing I came out here so often," thought Dencey, "or I might lose my path."

32. *Dencey under Concern*

SAMMIE JETSAM, lingering about the docks near eight o'clock of the evening for a last good-bye to friends, suddenly heard the South Church bell ring out wild and clanging. A fire! All Nantucket was in mortal fear of a fire. Even before the "great fire" of '46, this fire fear on the Island was intense. In this gale there'd be no downing it.

Sam's growing homesickness changed to delighted excitement. He jammed down his cap and ran up the street.

"Whar's the fire?" he demanded.

"I dunno," said the old sailmaker. "Must be out a ways. Folks is huntin' for it."

Jetsam ran onward. Up on State Street he caught at a hurrying man. "Whar's the fire?" he queried, amid the bell's loud clangor.

"'Tisn't a fire, sonny. It's that little girl of Lydia Coffyn's. She's lost."

"Lost! How—lost?" Something went wrong in Jetsam's chest. His throat shut tight.

174

"Dunno," said the citizen anxiously. "They're afraid she's drowned off the dock."

"She hain't." Jetsam heard somebody that might be himself asserting this. "She hain't no baby to go tumblin' off the dock."

"Hain't? How do ye know?"

"She hain't drowned, I tell ye." Sam seemed hitting out against some horror which could not be.

"Well, if ye know so much, go tell her mother."

Now the town crier came up the street ringing his bell.

"Child lost!" Cling—clang—cling—clang. "Child lost, Lydia Coffyn's Dionis. Had on a cloak an' a hood." Cling—clang. "Dionis Coffyn. Lost, lost."

Every stroke of his bell seemed to hit Sam in the same place in his chest that had gone wrong in the first place. The crying of Dencey's name like that on State Street was a curious offense. He wanted to choke Jake, the crier, and make him stop.

Without definite object, Jetsam began running toward North Water Street—toward the place he had last seen her. She must be there. She couldn't disappear. Anything as real and touchable as Dencey.

The Coffyn house loomed large and solid in the flying snow. All the lower windows shone with lights. Jetsam entered the yard and knocked timidly at the kitchen door. No one answered. He pushed the door open and peered in.

Peggy Runnel stood at the sink wringing out her dishcloth, wringing and wringing it and gazing at the window where already each little black pane was outlined in white clinging snow.

"So dark—so dark!" she moaned. "An' that child out in it. Oh—oh!"

She tossed down the dishcloth, went over to the fire-place, then back to the sink again. Sam was by this time in the middle of the room.

"Whar's she gone?" he demanded. "Whar's she gone, durn ye?"

Peggy Runnel stopped, aghast.

"Thee! Sam Jetsam! Thee! How dast thee show thy face here! The boldness o' it!"

"Tell me whar she is."

"And if we knew, wouldn't we go get her, Sam Jetsam? Is thee simple? Get out, I say. Lydia—Lydia," she lifted her voice and ran to the keeping-room door. "Hyar's that Sam Jetsam come to ax about Dencey. Of all things!"

Into the room came Lydia. Her face was white as chalk, and out of it her gray eyes shone like a wounded deer's. No one could have guessed that the low steady voice was controlling a fiery anger. She was frightened at her hatred of this mere boy.

"Please go away," she said. "We are very busy."

"I don't want nothin'. I jist want to know whar's Dencey. She hain't drowned," he asserted. "She hain't, I tell ye."

For answer, Lydia hurried to the kitchen door and opened it. A blast blew snow along the floor and flared up the fire under the pot.

"I cannot see thee now," she repeated, in her cold, even voice. "We are in great sorrow and thee is the cause."

Sam made no move toward the significant door.

"Me?" he shouted. "How'd I lose her?"

Suddenly the keeping-room door was thrown open again by Hedassah Gardner, full dressed in shaggy coat and muffler, and with a lighted tin lantern.

"We're all ready, Lydia," he said. "A posse of men is

searching the docks. Maggie Hall says she saw her about five o'clock going down that way, and a man saw her, too. But Ben and I are going out to the Commons. We'll find her—somewhere. Don't thee worry."

"I'm going with thee," she answered.

"Thee'd better not, Lydia. Thee might even delay us." They all hurried into the keeping-room, forgetting Jetsam entirely.

Peggy rushed to the door to close out the blast.

"Why doesn't thee go?" she demanded.

"What Mis' Coffyn mean sayin' I lost her?" insisted Sam.

" 'Cause thee did. The darling left a note pinned on her mother's pincushion and sayin', 'I'm under concern for Sammie Jetsam and have gone to find him!' Thee's always been enticin' her away, Sam Jetsam. An' now I reckon thee's killed her. Get out with thee!"

The door closed with a slam, leaving Sam in the whistling blackness and the snow.

"I'm under concern for Sammie Jetsam and have gone out to find him. I'm under concern for Sammie Jetsam." Over and over the words whirled in his brain like the whirling snow. So that's what she had done. "Under concern?" Yes, about what he had said this morning. That he was going with the showman. There was no harm in the showman. What a goose! How foolish girls were, anyway. Just because he teased her. Gone out to find him, had she, in this gale and snow. The fool! He was very angry with Dencey.

He stumbled out to the street. Two men came out the front door, bending double as they met the wind.

"I certainly hope the child hasn't gone to the Commons," said one. "The wind's gone around north. She might freeze; and with snow covering the roads, well, I don't see how on earth we're going to trace her. Of course, I didn't say that to Lydia."

"Thee didn't need to. She knows!" They hurried out of sight.

Jetsam ran ahead, passed them, and ran on toward Mill Hill and the Commons. Of course she'd gone there. That's where she always went to find him. He still thought he was angry.

"The goose," he kept saying, "the durned goose." But like a drowning refrain the words always came back. "I'm under concern for Sammie Jetsam. I'm under concern— I'm under——"

Sam understood the phrase. It was Quaker, and all Nantucket understood it. There was no stronger expression for earnest care and wish to help.

Under concern for Sammie Jetsam, yes, she'd been under that concern ever since she first came out on the Commons to find him. "She might 'a' know'd she'd git lost in this tarnal cold an' give all this trouble," he said. No, not even was she at fault there. It had been warmer this afternoon and had turned cold suddenly. It wasn't her fault. He couldn't fault her, try though he might. She'd just gone out to find him, like she always did. *Wonder what she brought him this time.* Suddenly, that giving of Dencey's, that continual giving, smote the boy horribly. She shouldn't give him nothin' more. Not a durn thing. He wouldn't take it from her.

When he passed Mill Hill into the open, the gale struck him and knocked him forward to his knees.

He scrambled up. Dencey was out in this. This gale, this snow, this blackness. Lordy! It would kill her, and she'd gone out for him—for him.

"Lord A'mighty," he couldn't find her this way. He was the fool, not she, to go out without a lantern. He must get a lantern—quick. He turned back facing the gale and, with the eerie sense of the very poor, found his way in the blackness down a little street and burst into a small hut.

"Gimme a lantern, Beppo," he shouted to the Portuguese, who sat crouched by the fire.

The family sprang up.

"What ye want, Sammé? Lantern? No go cabin to-night—stay here."

They were arguing with him. They laid hands upon him. Would they never understand?

"Gimme the lantern, I say. Give it me. Somebody's lost, I tell ye." He broke away from them, searching the house wildly himself.

"Maybe Meester Brown he go. He knows roads," they argued.

"I know the roads. Nobody knows 'em like me. She went out for me and it's me must find her. Oh——"

He had discovered the lantern himself. He opened it, saw the good long sperm candle, lighted it with a brand. Durn his fingers, what made them tremble so?

Then he slammed the door of the hut and was out in the night again. Very soon he met the full gale once more beyond Mill Hill on the open Commons. He pushed on in the buffeting darkness. His tin pierced lantern threw sprays of sparkles ahead of him on the snow. The road was already full of drifts—piled up against a straggling fence that ran along. Now the fence stopped. The road seemed to stop, too, only snow, snow, snow. Yes, Jetsam knew the roads, but he wished he could see Farmer Brown's light. He peered anxiously and made onward, blown fiercely forward by the wind. He knew the danger of the going.

33. *In the Storm*

SUCH A STRANGE thought crossed Jetsam. He had bargained with that girl Dencey for the book, the teaching, the food. He had all his life bargained for everything. But she would have given him all those things and taken nothing. Bargaining meant nothing to her. She'd give anyway. Why? Durn it, he didn't know. He reckoned she was a fool. Give and git nothin'. And now she'd given the last thing. Maybe she was dead—for him, for him!

Lordy, how his throat hurt!

He stopped and swung his lantern wrathfully.

Couldn't he stop that fool thinking? He'd miss the road himself, if he didn't watch out.

Then a blessing. Quite suddenly he saw, far off in a waste of snow, the mist-sprayed gleam of Farmer Brown's light. He took his bearings by it. The road turned here. Yes, his lantern caught the stunted tree he knew. He knew the road. He could follow somehow. But Dencey—of course she couldn't find it. Give and git nothin'. Give and git nothin'. Whar was she? Half buried in a drift, most like.

181

The snow was up to his calves now. He had to push through it like a plow. All the way he watched for signs of Dencey. But he saw no signs. The snow covered everything. Of course, she would try to get to Jill's cabin. He would find her there.

If he was crying, he was spared the shame of it, for the snow was so thick on his eyelashes and wet on his face that even he could not have told.

He passed the second farmhouse far to the left—a glimmering beacon. Oh, if he could go faster. Never, never had the way been so long.

At last Jill's hut. It was Jetsam's first instinct to hide from Jill. She might stop him. He stole up noiselessly and peeped into the flake-laden window. There Jill sat before a fresh fire—crouched on the floor. No one else was in the cabin. Suddenly, Jill looked around with that strange sixth sense she had.

"Daggon't—she could allus tell if anybody was near. She was an Injun, sure enough."

He stole back, hiding behind the wood-shed. All was still. He did not want to look into the shed. That was the last chance of finding Dencey. It took all his courage to make the test.

He looked.

Dencey was not there!

The ache in Jetsam's throat suddenly became a wild terror. She was gone—gone—gone. He had searched carefully all along the way, he had come to the goal. Beyond this was doubt. Miles of doubt. She might be anywhere on the Island. Behind him, before him. Buried in the snow. Dead!

("I am under concern for Sammie Jetsam.")

"She done it for me,"—Jetsam's half-frozen lips formed the words.

There is no heart-tug in the world so strong as this thought. Whole religions have been founded upon it and lasted alive through a thousand years. The thought swept the poor waif of a boy stronger than the gale and the storm. It swept the ignorance out of his mind and the fear out of his will.

He ran out of the wood-shed holding his arms high in front of him.

"Say, looky here," he shouted. "I got to find her. She'll die ef I don't. Ye see that, don't ye? I've gotta find her *quick*, too. Do ye hear?"

Who was to hear, Jetsam didn't know. It wasn't a prayer, it was a threat. It hadn't even the bargaining of Jacob, but it had strength. His mind went suddenly clear and unafraid. He walked toward the road swinging his lantern to throw its light as far as might be. Then he turned back again, past the house, and down toward the hollow where he chopped wood. He kept the lantern close to the ground. Abruptly the sparkles showed something—black lump. He pulled it out of the snow.

It was Dencey's school bag. Hope shouted all through him. He crouched low over the lantern. Yes, footprints, footprints almost covered. Jetsam began to tremble so he could hardly hold the lantern. He knelt in the snow—bringing his face close. Yes, they were little footprints—not Jill's. There was another—another. Oh, Lord! he mustn't miss them.

Suddenly, Wash the dog dashed through the drifts into the circle of light—leaping and yelping. Jetsam seized him and rubbed his nose in the tracks.

"Sick 'em—sick 'em, Wash. Find 'er. Here, come along."

Track by track they followed.

Now they lost them.

Wash went sniffing wildly around in the snow. Jetsam gave himself a sharp hit in the chest, so sharp that it hurt.

"Find them tracks agin, ye fool," he said. But it was not he who found them, but Wash.

The tracks began to be plainer. Jetsam realized that it had stopped snowing. He could not tell when it had stopped. He began to halloo: "Dencey—Dencey Coffyn, com-hyar—com-hyar," but the wind caught the sound and whipped it to naught.

Still the tracks. Goshamighty, how fur had she come, anyway? He must be almost to Hummock Pond. He could hear the breakers beyond Ram Pasture. The tracks were leading down to the pond. Would she fall in?

Wash, ahead in the darkness, gave one terrific yelp. In suffocating wonder, Jetsam dashed after him.

Was this Dencey? Such a strange object—crouched in a ball like a cat, wrapped in her coat, her big bonnet hiding her.

Jetsam seized her arm and dragged her up to her feet. Perfectly limp she was, falling back to the snow.

"Dencey," he called. "Dencey!" For one wild moment he thought she was dead. Then came a faint moan, and Jetsam sat her down and began to slap her cheeks and lift her arms.

"Don't, Jetsam," she said mildly. "I'm so sleepy."

"Ye're freezin'-sleepy," he shouted. "Wake up. Darn ye, Dencey—wake up!"

He slapped her rudely, fiercely, and suddenly, to his overwhelming joy, she slapped him back—a good sound slap, too.

"Thee stop that, Sam Jetsam."

"No, I won't stop. Not till ye're plumb awake. Kin ye stand now? Oh, but yer teeth is chatterin'. Yer awful cold. Ain't ye?"

"Yes." She began to cry. "Oh, Jetsam, where are we?"

Yes—where were they? The blackness of their situation suddenly made his teeth chatter, too—with terror. Hummock Pond? He was almost sure they were there. And if so, there wasn't a soul near, not a house for miles. Jill's cabin was the nearest, and that three miles away. Could he carry Dencey? He feared not. Dencey was no sylph. She weighed heavier than he. If he failed, it would mean death to both of them. He stood in a puzzle.

Then he remembered a sheep shelter that was on the edge of Hummock Pond. It was for the protection of sheep in just such weather as this. It wasn't much, open all of one side. But Jim Sears used it for a hunting covert. Once Jetsam had been with him there three days to help him. Could he find it now in the blackness? He couldn't leave Dencey to search for it. That was certain.

She was sitting down again.

"Git up," he shouted angrily. "Ye want to die, Dence Coffyn? There, now. Come with me."

He pulled her to her feet, and with one arm about her, the other holding his lantern, started forward. He had only gone a few feet when he stumbled and fell flat.

He got up swearing, seized his lantern, which luckily was still alight, and kicked the object angrily.

Then suddenly he stopped kicking.

"Oh, Lord, my wood-pile!" he cried out.

"Thy wood-pile?" queried Dencey.

"Yes, Lordy, Lordy! Don't ye see? Hit's the wood I brung for Jim this fall. We're near the sheep shelter. That's sure."

He clutched Dencey and started forward again. The exercise began to revive Dencey. She remembered.

"Oh, Jetsam, don't go with the showman!" she wailed.

"Do I look like it?" he answered wrathfully.

"But why are we taking all these walks? It isn't a good place to walk."

But just at this moment their feet splashed into the skim-frozen water. Jetsam bent down and tasted it. It was fresh.

"I know now," he shouted. "Hit's Hummock Pond. I got my bearin's."

He listened keenly to catch the sound of the surf which he knew was south of the pond. Then made his way along the water's edge. A few feet, and the lantern sparkled upon the crazy hut buried in the snow. He pulled Dencey around to the open front of it.

Well, it wasn't so bad. The snow had swirled in a drift all one end. But the other end was clear. And the walls and roof kept off the worst of the wind. Three sheep were huddled in the dry corner. He pushed Dencey up against them.

"They'll warm ye," he said.

Then, anxiously, hurriedly, he began to search the hut. Jim generally left things here to come back to. Yes, here was the tinder box where Jim always kept it, and a heap of dry grass. Hurriedly, too, he brought in some of the wood. Dencey did not offer to help him. He knew she was stupefied with cold.

Then at last he lighted the fire. The forsaken place leaped into visibility, life, and warmth—warmth.

But the sheep were frightened and stumbled baa-ing out into the night.

"Oh, the poor sheep," sobbed Dencey. But she crouched close to the fire, warming her hands.

"These three fingers don't feel anything at all," she commented. And Jetsam hastened to rub them with snow until sharp pains ran through them. And Dencey began to cry again. Oh, he wished she weren't so sleepy, sitting there by the fire. He wished there were more wood.

He went to the opening and peered out. Yes, it was as he had thought. The storm was clearing, great scudding clouds driving from the north and the wind like a thousand devils. Getting colder every minute. He must hurry for dear life. He went back to Dencey.

"Dencey," he said, "I got to go back an' tell the folks so they'll come an' git ye. Try not to go to sleep, Dencey, for God's sake, try. An' here's some dry wood—keep puttin' it on the fire."

"I don't want to be alone," quavered Dencey. "Don't thee go and leave me alone."

Jetsam shook her angrily. "Try to understand. I got to go 'cause it's gittin' colder an' we ain't got dry wood. An' the stars is out, I can find my way. Ye won't be alone, anyway," he added quickly. "Here's Wash, he'll stay with ye."

"Lie down, Wash. Lie down thar." The dog with a reluctant whine lay close to Dencey.

Then, with one anxious look at both of them, Jetsam hurried out.

Oh, a long, long way under fitful stars. Now they swam in mad race, as the swift clouds passed them. Now were lost in the fleece, now popped out bright and clear again. How well he knew them and their stations over the wide moor. And the moon, too, was rising.

All this was to his good. But not the cold.

The cold was a fierce enemy and the wind a fighter. It came out of the north and struck him in the face. It searched his jacket and his shirt and made them as naught. The whole front of him seemed naked to the wind. He must push into it faster—faster. Dencey didn't want to be alone. What if she let the fire die out? Oh, hurry, hurry!

He must have passed Jill's cottage by now. If only he wouldn't go so slow. Always slower. He fell down and scrambled up again on perfectly stilt-like legs, pushed on again with feet that were two lumps of ice and didn't want to move.

Again he fell, again got up and faced the wind. Then came Farmer Brown's light far over there on the other road. Brown always kept a light on a night like this. And at last, at last, the lights of town windows, the blessed streets of town.

It was two o'clock of the morning, but the Coffyn house was all alight. Alight with activity and sorrow.

Hedassah Gardner had come back almost frozen. He had been out to Jill's cottage. Everybody was thinking, "The child is dead by now." Everybody said cheerily, "We'll find her. We won't give up."

Mrs. Coffyn sat alone by the keeping-room fire, stony still with hands hard-clasped. Always the words of telling Tom this thing when he came home. As if she didn't care about Dencey, but only about telling Tom.

"Tom, I didn't take care of thy daughter, not right care. She got lost in the Commons. Yes, Tom she's——" Then the words stopped and began over again, and kept her from praying.

Peggy Runnel, in the kitchen, was getting breakfast. Of course, it was night yet, but she had to do something.

Then the door banged open without a knock and Jetsam's ragged figure was in the middle of the kitchen.

"I've found her. Whar's Mis' Coffyn?" said his queer, strained voice.

"Ye've found what? Thee!" Peggy's contempt denied it.

"Yes, I did, too. She's out on the Commons."

"Dead—dead!" screamed Peggy and went, laughing and crying all at once, to the keeping room.

Lydia rushed into the kitchen.

Jetsam stepped close to her.

"Listen to me," he shouted, "an' don't ye act like this hyar fool. I found her. I found Dencey."

Lydia's spirit beat upward in an instant psalm. "Oh, thank God—thank God!"

"Keep still, will ye?" said Jetsam with threatening hands uplifted. "Ye must be quick—listen."

Lydia seized the hands and held them—a gesture she had with her own children.

"What is thee sayin?" she demanded. "Thee found her? Was she—she—?"

"No—I tell ye. She was livin'. She's in that sheep shelter o' Jim Sears', the second one this side o' Hummock Pond. Not the first one. Do ye hyar?"

"Yes, yes, I hear, thee need not scream." Joy flooded Lydia's face as she leaned toward him.

"An' there was a leetle firewood, an' I wrapped her in a ole blanket. Hit was awful dirty, ma'am. But hit was all they was."

"Yes, yes, child." Lydia put her arm about the thin shoulders, but he struggled away.

"But the fire'll die down. She's too near froze to tend it. Ef it does, she'll die, too. Do ye hyar?" Hoarser and hoarser his voice. Would his teeth lock with chattering so he could not speak? "Come along. I'll show ye the way. Ye don't dast mistake it. Hit's the second hut, not the fust. Hurry. Hurry."

He pulled her rudely.

"We'll find it, child. Hedassah knows," said Lydia.

She saw a look of wild relief spring into the boyish face. He went ashen pale, and his shoulders hunched upward in helpless shaking and quivering.

Lydia ran to the next room and, reaching with a long stick out the window, knocked loudly on the window next door.

Martha White's frightened face appeared.

"What is it?—Oh, is she—?"

"No—no. She's found. Come quick and tend the boy. He's in a hard chill by the kitchen fire. Hot foot bath and the cordial in the kitchen closet. Quick!"

Lydia did not wait for coat and hat, but ran out of the house and down the snowy street to Hedassah Gardner's.

34. *Sammie Jetsam in Limbo*

DIONIS, TOUGH AS a little moor pine, was none the worse for her adventure. She sat wrapped in three blankets by the fire all day and drank hot soup and enjoyed being a heroine. And when, the following morning, the boys pounded on her door, she had no thought of oversleeping her breakfast.

But Jetsam lay in the little room off the kitchen tossing and muttering with fever. And by nightfall had entered the dread limbo of a serious illness.

"Dencey," he would call hoarsely. "Dencey Coffyn—com-hyar—"

But when she came, frightened and wild-eyed, he did not know her at all. Then he would swear strange oaths flavored with the sea and rip out the language of Dicky Dicks, so that Lydia would send her daughter hastily from the room.

All the while Lydia's pale purity bent over him, apparently not hearing the wild obscenities. Always through Lydia's mind marched the remembrance of her run down the street to Hedassah Gardner's and how she was in heaven then. Tom need not be told that his daughter was dead. Dencey lived. This boy had lifted her from hell into that heaven. Her heart still sang with it. She never forgot.

Lydia was very busy. She washed the boy from head to foot, wrung out hot flaxseed poultices for his chest, cooled his face with water. At times she held his hot, hard little hands trying to comfort him.

"But don't ye hyar 'er callin'?" he would argue. "She's dyin', durn ye! Dencey's dyin' an' ye won't leave me go to her."

"Dencey is well," she told him, with tears suddenly stinging her eyes. "It was only thy-self cried out just now. There—be still."

"Oh, Mother"—Dionis would catch at her mother's dress hastening through the kitchen—"is he—is he goin' to die?"

"I do not know. He is very ill."

"But," Dionis wailed, "he will die in sin. He hired himself to the showman. He hasn't repented."

Her mother stopped sternly.

"What does thee know of repentance, Dionis? He forgot the show and all its vanities to go out and save thee from the storm. Sometimes there are martyr spirits among us and we do not see."

Dencey, somewhat stunned at the sudden change in her mother, watched her disappear into the darkened room.

It was a terrible illness—lung fever, so the doctor called it. Jetsam did not rally but went down and down. The poor ill-nourished body had no weapons to fight the strong disease. The starved mind and ill-conditioned spirit had but a lax hold on life. Injun Jill's wrath, lonely pathways across the moors, wood-chopping in the bitter wood-shed, rough usage by the sailors, anger, cheating, sudden fights by dirty candlelight—these peopled the boy's mind.

"Look out thar," he would warn Lydia, flinging out an arm. "The man's got a knife. Lordy, whad I tell ye? Ye fool! Whad I tell ye?"

So the young desolate mind unfolded itself before Lydia. The slow weeks went by and she tended the skeleton-like body with tears of pity running down her cheeks.

"He has had no chance—no chance," she murmured. "He will go out of life knowing nothing."

She began to pray for the waif as though he had been her own flesh and blood.

Meanwhile, to Dionis, going back and forth to school, life seemed abruptly changed and empty. Jetsam was in trouble and she had nothing to do with it. She couldn't bear to go into the strange sick-room. Yet all the while she kept feeling as she did that time she pulled out her loose tooth. Something gone—yet something hurt.

It had been a great burden going out to the Commons to teach Jetsam and to get him things to eat. Now Mother had taken all that burden. And yet Dionis was mad at Mother.

Injun Jill was mad, too. She came to the back door begging and pleading to see Jetsam.

"Gif pack my booy," she said angrily. "He mine. Mine."

Mother's eyes flashed.

"If he is thine, thee has strangely abused him. Go away. Thee shall not frighten the poor lad."

"Ye got doozen childrenth," declared Injun Jill. "An' ye coom dake mine, mine. Ye no Christian. Ye heathen." She flung her two hands wildly above her head.

Then Mother threatened her with the sheriff. Injun Jill went away, stamping and crying. Injun Jill, bereft of all her power.

And now Dionis was sorry for Injun Jill and mad at Mother. What for? Dionis had the unchancy experience of seeing abysses in her own soul.

Meanwhile, up and down Nantucket everybody was calling Dencey "good." Everybody knew that "Lydia's Dencey" had gone out into the storm on the Commons to save a boy's soul. "Who had ever thought that Dionis Coffyn was so religious? Why, she seemed of frivolous conversation. Well, thee never can tell."

But Dionis didn't feel "good." Hadn't she broken her promise to Aunt Lovesta in going out on the Commons?

What did they mean?

Then came the most horrible day of all, when the littlest children were sent over to Martha White's and everybody went about the house whispering because they thought Sammie Jetsam was going to die.

35. *Jetsam Discovers the Coffyns*

IF JETSAM, IN THE fullness of vigor and suffi-
ciency had entered into the Coffyn family, no doubt
he would have flung out again the first day. The decorum,
the pious phrases, the regularity would have been impossible. But he came to it by way of suffering and silence.

The first time he awoke, he did not know where he
was. The room was dim. He was aware of feeling very
smooth and cool all over his skin—a kind of silkiness.
Jetsam had never been really clean before, and he was not
at all sure he liked it. The second time he awoke, someone in a white cap bent over him and said, "God be
thanked, thee is better."

This struck Jetsam as terribly embarrassing.

"Don't say that thar," he murmured.

"Why not, dear child?"

"'Cause hit's silly. Me and God!"

"My dear, my dear," said the shocked Lydia.

As time went on, he realized that the person who moved
so softly about the room was Mrs. Coffyn. He was afraid.
He had always run away when she appeared. He couldn't

run now. Jetsam had suffered much in his short life. He had always suffered alone, drooping and muffled like a hurt bird until the visitation be past. Now he would waken with pain in the most unexpected places. Lydia's invasion upon it was only one more pain to bear. She gave him a hot drink, rubbed his bony back with lard, the gentle hand going up and down, up and down. The pain retired.

And suddenly, in Jetsam's hard cold world, was a new thing—tender, brooding, like an unbelievable dawn to one who had never seen the sunrise. Ah, warm, living, immeasurable. Lydia, as she turned away, felt herself suddenly clutched in a wildling embrace; and the boy's sobbing frightened her.

Only a moment, and Jetsam never did it again, but from that moment Jetsam began to mend.

Soon he was able to come out by the great kitchen fire with its generous roar of heat and its back log like ancient Yule. Strange for a boy who had always snatched a cold breakfast anyhow, under the snarls of Injun Jill, to see the Coffyn family gather, happy and orderly, about their board. First the silent grace. Then the hearty eating. Such a plenty of everything and never a morning when there was nothing. Little Ariel was given a bowl of porridge to bring to him, and he so proud of the duty.

"Aw, he can't do it," spoke up Kanah. "He's too little."

"He's not too little to learn kindness," answered Lydia. And Dionis came to steady the baby steps.

After breakfast came the long Silence which certainly seemed foolish to Jetsam. All heads bowed in a compact of family love and aspiring. Sometimes the boys wiggled, or Ariel got up and wandered among them. Jetsam watched it all—the quiet faces, the immovable white caps of Lydia, Peggy, and Jane, the clock ticking so solemnly in its corner, the fire snapping softly to itself. The deep, deep absorption. A strange foolishness, surely.

Then, suddenly, chairs rasped back. Everybody rushed away to wood-chopping, sweeping, dishes—the same duty for the same child every day. Then, like a departing whirlwind, the youngsters went to school.

Now Jetsam was well enough to be promoted to the keeping room. It was Dencey's part to wait while the others were at supper and tend the keeping-room fire, and set the chairs about in a generous circle for everybody. After supper they gathered in.

"Draw into the circle," Lydia would say cheerily. "It's cold to-night."

And soon they were all busy at something. The boys doing lessons. Jane with her splendid silk quilt all of gray and white pieces. Dencey telling a story to Ariel that made his eyes pop with wonder. Sometimes the boys fell to quarreling, and Lydia sent them to bed. But, of course, they retired to the back yard and had it out. Or Peggy teased Stephen till he lost his temper, or the children quarreled over their play and Lydia meted out mistaken justice always favoring the youngest. But spite of all, it was a room of peace and trust, a room that was piling up memories into a preciousness that would flower some day into generous deeds and sturdy virtue.

Jetsam watched all this in silence. Jill's cabin, with its old bitterness, its chilling fear, seemed on some other planet. He felt weightless and light in his freedom from it.

Sometimes Jetsam put wood on the fire, sometimes he showed the boys a new rig for their boats. But, for the most part, he was overwhelmed with shyness, a fish out of water. The boy who had been the "baddest boy in town" was afraid to speak.

And always he was uncomfortably aware that he was missing something. He had not caught the clue!

Then, one afternoon, the household happiness was augmented. Captain Coffyn's ship was reported in near-by waters. Everybody bustled about in expectation, and that night Captain Coffyn came into the room like a splendid breeze. His face was the bright shining tan of those who are just come off the sea, his hat and coat were covered with snow.

Lydia sprang up with a low, instinctive cry—the same sound, Jetsam noted, that she had uttered that night when he told her of Dencey. She ran to him and helped him off with his coat, Stephen took his dripping hat. Then they brought him to the fire.

"But it's too hot," cried Tom. "It isn't really cold outside."

How they waited upon him, bringing in a generous supper so he could eat in their midst. Ariel climbed into his lap asking over and over, "Is it really Father?" Dionis hung upon his shoulder and kissed him whenever she brought him a dish.

"I'm going to stay," he told her, " a good long while, this time. Thee can tell that to the King o' the Whales. I know he'll be glad."

"We are the ones to be glad," said Lydia softly.

Then indeed did peace settle down over the busy household, as into it entered the abiding love of Lydia and Tom Coffyn. Lydia became sweetly young as she went about her tasks. Tom was the life of everything. The children took no accounting of this love. But it was there, and each one unconsciously basked in it, breathed it like the air. Each child, even Peggy in the kitchen, was fed and nourished by it.

And strangely, too, it fed their faith. Something seemed to sweep the human love into higher spaces, where it breathed the air of the love of God.

More and more did the shy, starved Sammie Jetsam know that something was eluding him—some richness in which he had no part.

36. *Hunger of the Mind*

I T WASN'T AS though Jetsam had not always been hungry. Hungry for bread, hungry for the things beyond bread, the relationships of life, father, mother, the "belonging" to anybody. Hungry for the dim Something beyond even this, which might be called a boy's God.

He remembered one bitter evening last winter when he had been creeping toward Dicky Dicks's, fearful lest Dicky should refuse him shelter. He had met Zeke Severance (Hopestill's brother) going whistling up the street toward his big comfortable home on North Water Street, his hearth fire and warm supper. And on the way to all that he was eating a huge piece of pie.

In blind wrath, Jetsam had sprung at him, knocked the pie out of his hand and a front tooth out of his mouth. Then he threw the pie into the gutter and went and hid behind Dicky's bar, too miserable even to cry. The dim things he wanted clutched him so he could scarcely breathe.

And now, here in the Coffyn household, was that same keen taste in his mind. A precious thing, such hunger—

almost worth the starvation to produce it.

The Coffyn household had its mental interests, all the more real for being so casual. They centered in Tom. Tom brought back the world into the home. He told of the snowy, soaring peaks of the Andes, the curious beliefs of the Chinese, the religious ceremonies in South Pacific islands. But most of all he told of flowers. He had his book of pressed tropical plants and spent his evenings classifying them. Sometimes he would stop to recount how he had found some flower, his narrow escapes in jungle or island as he searched. He told of curious animals.

"But in New Holland is a whole class of animals utterly different from those of any continent. Why should that be? There's a puzzle for thee," he said eagerly, pinching Dencey's cheek.

This was all new to Jetsam. The rough sailors and Portugese brought no such tidings as this to Dicky Dicks's fireside: the new scientific point of view which Jetsam's crude mind caught, recognizing the expanding life of it. It was to be the growing thought of his own generation. The Severance boys listened also, and Dencey crowded close, her eyes like dark lakes.

Of a surety, Jetsam's hunger was being fed.

At this time Stephen Grellet, the famous Quaker preacher, came on his religious visit to the Island. He was the Coffyn's guest—a little thin-faced man with a prominent nose, who spoke with a French accent and gestured eagerly. But how his face shone! He told of forest journeys in Tennessee where they lashed two canoes together and set the wheels of the carriage in them to cross the river. He and his companion had met panthers, bears, and wolves on that journey. They had eaten only two small corn cakes a day, and the horses ate young twigs and leaves. "My dear Master was pleased to bring me through all these difficulties," he said.

Grellet had met King Bernadotte of Sweden, had been in the midst of his gorgeous court. He had sat on a sofa with the Emperor of all the Russias, prayed with him, and told him of the sufferings of his (the Emperor's) people so that the Emperor promised to relieve them. He told of Constantinople, Smyrna, and the Ægean Islands.

Jetsam sat listening in complete delight, drawn to this interesting, fearless, and loving little man.

Oh, if he only knew whether the Coffyns would let him stay! No one had said he might, and he dared not ask even Dencey.

And there was always the background of Injun Jill. Indeed, she was more than background. He was still quite weak and daunted with illness when, one morning in the kitchen, he looked up and she was there—Injun Jill with her same old coat, her same cruel domination.

"Ye coom wid me. My booy, darn ye! Coom, I tell ye." And with the old familiar oath she grabbed him with both her hands.

Jetsam wrenched himself free and fled. Fled through the cold front hall up the front stairs to Lydia's room. He burst in upon her, she on her knees, threw arms about her, almost knocking her backward.

"Don't let her take me," he panted. "I can't hit her hard enough now."

Lydia loosened his clasp and rose up, straightening her cap.

"Thee should not come in now," she said severely. Then, seeing his pleading face, she added:

"Thee stay here. I will deal with Injun Jill."

Crouching in the bare gray room, Jetsam heard Lydia go down the stairs. Heard her clear commands and Injun Jill's angry outbursts. Then the back door opened, and Jill, breathing out threatening and slaughter, went down the street.

It was several nights after this rescue. The youngsters had all gone to bed. Tom was away, having gone on some personal business to New York. Lydia was carefully covering the great kitchen fire with ashes. Then she rose from her knees, took the last candle from the mantel, and started toward the door.

"Thee must go to bed now," she told Jetsam. "Thee mustn't linger after the others are gone."

Jetsam seemed to force his lips to speak.

"Mis' Coffyn—be I well now?"

"Thee must say 'am I'—not 'be I.' Yes, thee is well. Thee has only coughed a few times to-day."

"Mis' Coffyn, I made up them coughs, made 'em every time ye come int' the room."

"Made them up!" Lydia's candle slanted, dripping the sperm. "What does thee mean?"

"I don't want to be well. I don't. I'd ruther be sick." He turned his back upon her going over to the warm hearth as if with that old instinct of the suppliant.

"I wisht I could stay sick," he repeated.

"That is wicked." Lydia came and put her candle back on the mantel prepared to labor with this strange child. "God made thee well, and prayer to God."

He could hardly speak now for the hurried breaths in his throat.

"No, it hain't wicked," he broke out. " 'Cause if I could

stay sick I could stay hyar."

"But thee is to stay here anyway. Why!" said Lydia, astonished. "Didn't thee understand that? Did thee suppose after thee saved Dionis's life we would send thee away?"

The boy knelt down, stretching out his hands over the warm ashes. He did not speak, but Lydia saw that his hands trembled and his teeth were chattering as if with chill.

"Of course, thee'll have to earn thy keep," she said thriftily. "Even Stephen's boys do that."

"I kin airn my keep," he said with unsteady lips. "I allus done that, ever sence I could walk."

37. *The Committee on Sufferings*

JETSAM SLEPT LITTLE that night. He lay awake in a floating dream, the happiness of the poet when some new poem is spreading a lighted mist throughout his mind. He thought of them all in the big house lying in their separate beds and he in his bed, his own now, warm, shut in from the world. He loved them all, Stephen so fine mannered, Ariel who climbed on his lap and called him "my Jeshum," Captain Tom, and the white-kerchiefed Lydia.

But of them all it was Dencey whom his mind singled out to dream upon. Dencey was his own. He knew her ways and she knew his. He had saved her from freezing in the Commons. Mrs. Coffyn had said so. A great glow of pride went over him.

And from this grand house Dencey had come out on the Commons to teach him. Strange for her to do that. But it was because of her home she came. Dencey interpreted it, and it interpreted Dencey. He sighed and turned over in bed.

"It was Dencey done it," he said aloud, and suddenly Dencey's sunburned face swam before him, her dancing, merry eyes.

Young as he was, one might say he fell in love with Dencey that night. That was too bad. His chances would have been so much better if he hadn't done it.

In this night, too, was born Jetsam's loyalty, and that was no mean creature. What the Coffyns did was the norm. What the Coffyns wished must be performed. What the Coffyns believed—well, it was all right for them to be Quakers. But he wouldn't be. It was too blame foolish.

And the very next morning he saw Quakerism at its worst. The Committee on Sufferings arrived at the house.

Five men and five women, Aunt Susanna the self-constituted head, filed into the keeping room. They were as forbidding a decemvirate as could well be found, the men frowning under their broad hats, the women with shawls exactly adjusted (it took hours to do it), their arms folded in the shawls, their lips pressed into straight lines. So did their errand brand them.

"Well, Lydia," said Susanna. "We have come to look at thy belongings. They say thy floor coverings are not what they should be."

Peggy peeked into the keeping room.

"Drat'em," she murmured. Peggy, too, was loyal.

"What'll they do?" whispered Jetsam, glancing in at Lydia's troubled face.

"Do! Thee'll see. They'll do enough. The ole Squelchin' Committee. Last year they pulled up all Judy Swain's larkspurs 'cause they said they was too blue."

They came into the kitchen and inspected the dishes.

"Thank goodness, I'd jist washed 'em," was Peggy's comment.

They looked at the window curtains and upstairs at the bed draperies. Blue was a worldly colour and taboo. In the keeping room they found a chair with a mahogany rose on the back, and whipped out a chisel and hammer which they always carried, and promptly removed it.

Lydia's face was a picture, and Jetsam would have liked to fly at them and scratch them.

Then in the best parlor they found what they had come for—a crimson carpet. They withdrew their steps from it.

"I am astonished at thee, Friend Lydia," spoke Liakim Cole. "Thee must have this vain and worldly thing removed before next Monthly Meeting."

Lydia's face went perfectly white.

"I shall not remove it, Friend Liakim," she answered.

"Thee must. Does thee wish the Monthly Meeting to deal with thee?"

"No, I hope it will not."

"Then thee will remove it?"

"No."

Aunt Susanna seized her arm. "What on earth does thee mean, Lydia? I never knew that worldly things had such a hold on thee."

Lydia suddenly flushed as red as she had been white.

"It is not the thing," she said. "It is the gift. My husband gave me this the day he came home this time. If I destroy it, it will be in disobedience and ingratitude to my husband. Tell that to the Monthly Meeting."

They said little further. They seemed to know Lydia. And a few moments later she held open the door for them to file out.

Pathetic figures. This desperate care always means just one thing—that the living faith is waning. Already, in those days in Nantucket, the strong, soul-freshening vision of Quakerism was growing dim. These were they who knew its adorable preciousness, and they were trying to snatch it back into life. Prohibitions, "shalt-nots," and punishments were to protect the heavenly thing.

They knew not that life could be renewed only with more life.

Out in the kitchen, Jetsam was planning with Peggy. "Ef they come agin, we kin fight 'em," he said breathlessly. "Steve's as big as a man, an' I'm feisty now. Even Kanah he could bite 'em."

"Don't thee dare to say that to Mis' Coffyn. She don't believe in fightin'. She's fur peace. All the same, they won't git the floor-coverin', mark my word."

Jetsam and Dionis came into the keeping room where Lydia was nervously replacing the Chinese rose jars on the mantel. Even the children could see that she was cut to the quick. Jetsam, longing to do so, dared not speak, but Dionis ventured.

"Mother, I'm sorry they broke thy chair," she said.

"Child," answered Lydia bitterly, "we can be glad if they do not break somebody's heart."

38. *Going Before Her Guide*

THE "HEART" LYDIA spoke of was none other than Aunt Lovesta's. Being an adult heart, the young folk took little account of it. Jetsam indeed saw something of the truth, but Dionis could not realize that anybody could break anything about Aunt Lovesta.

Jetsam was sitting in his little room reading. He read every book he could get hold of—even almanacs. The door of the kitchen was open, and he saw Lovesta Coffyn come in. She said:

"Lydia, stop thy work a minute. I want to talk with thee."

Lydia turned anxiously.

"Oh, Lovesta, has it come?" she asked.

"Yes. I fear so."

Lydia took her hands out of the dough, washed them carefully, and came over to the fire.

"I had to seek thee," Lovesta said with a disturbedness which no one had ever seen upon her face. "I've taken it to the Lord. That should be enough. But I get no peace. It is as if I could not breathe. At last I seem to be clear to come to thee."

But, having got so far, Lovesta did not proceed. She sat slowly twisting her hands together—those hands which were usually so quiet.

"Did they accuse thee outright?" asked Lydia's awed voice.

Jetsam looked up from his reading. He had always listened to whatever he wanted to hear. He had always known Nantucket news as soon as the town crier.

"Yes, they visited me this morning. The whole Committee on Sufferings. Susanna is very severe. She says—they all say," she choked a little, "that I go before my Guide."

Of course, Jetsam did not understand this. What did she mean? The mystery fascinated him.

"How can they dare!" broke out the indignant Lydia. "Thee with thy power of the Spirit. It is outrageous!"

Lovesta looked down at her hands.

"The worst of it is," she said dully, "it is true—that is, it was true once. This is my punishment."

"Lovesta, what is thee saying? It can't be. Why, thy testimony last First Day. The Power was in it, flowing over us all. And hearts were tendered. There was Noah Swain, who never before—"

Lovesta's face lighted. "Yes, the Lord was with me last First Day," she said. "The watering was from above. I felt the Divine ease. *I* did nothing."

"It was only once," she added. "Almost a year ago at Yearly Meeting: It was such a full meeting—so many from the Cape and Rhode Island"—her head went down. "I wanted them to honour our Gay Street meeting. We had had so many and such long silences—dull ones. I can al-

ways find words, Lydia, and I was tempted—and spoke.
I—I—went before my Guide—that once."

Jetsam leaned forward, his eyes fixed. What was this
thing they were so sure they had and so sure they hadn't?
It made his flesh creep.

"Yes," agreed Lydia after a horrified silence. "I remember that testimony. I thought it was my fault that it seemed
so bare of the Spirit."

"It was bare of the Spirit and richened by Beelzebub,"
Lovesta accused herself. "But I have never done it since. I
repented—repented day long and night long. I did not
speak in meeting again for months—thee knows. Nay,
even when the Spirit urged me, I held back until at last
the forgiveness was sure. Peace and Life flowed so I could
on no account stop them. The Lord has loosed me from
my bonds."

She looked up. It was not the firelight made her face
shine so strangely.

Jetsam was frightened. He remembered what Dionis
had said about Jesus speaking to Aunt Lovesta. Evidently
it was true. He wanted to shut the door but he did not
dare.

"Indeed, indeed, thee has borne testimony," said Lydia.
"Never such rich testimony as thee does now."

Lovesta's light quenched like a snuffed candle.

"Susanna says I shall not speak again. The Committee
will report to the Monthly Meeting. I may not even speak
next First Day. Lydia, it will kill me."

"How dare they quench the Spirit! They sha'n't do it,"
Lydia said doggedly.

"But they will," said Lovesta. "I confessed to them as I
have to thee. But they say I go before my Guide every

First Day, and—and that I must acknowledge that before they will pardon me. They say I use many and strange words they never heard—that I make up my sentences beforehand. I do not. I do not."

Lovesta began to tremble. "Lydia, I cannot bear it," she burst out. "I tell thee I cannot bear it!" And Aunt Lovesta, the strong, broke down completely, bowing her capped head, hiding her sobbing face in her hands.

39. *Someone Is Hungry*

THE COMMITTEE ON Sufferings forbade Lovesta Coffyn to preach. The cruelty of their decision was perhaps unknown to themselves. They none of them had the "preaching spirit" which Lovesta possessed. They knew not what it meant, that sealing of the fountain of expression, that shutting in of a power whose nature was to come forth, which so imprisoned could break the heart.

The report of the Committee came up in Monthly Meeting, and spite of the best efforts of Lovesta's friends, the interdict was signed. Her minute was taken away. She could no longer go to any city and speak, for the interdiction was reported everywhere. She could no longer follow her instinct of loving solicitude for those far away. She no longer could be soul-lighted with enterprise.

Thus began Lovesta's long silence, so well known in the annals of Nantucket, as it is also known that, after twenty-five years, the decision was rescinded, and Lovesta bloomed once more with the Divine word. She had a concern to preach in Scandinavia and traveled from end to end of the Scandinavian peninsula, speaking the words of life.

But now, in these first tragic days, Lovesta kept her house. She was shamed before the world. But her chief suffering was not shame but suffocation. She began to lose flesh. She would not eat. She lived quite alone. Her husband had been killed in a battle with a whale in the South Pacific, her two young sons had shipped last year on a whaling voyage.

Lydia went to her and pleaded for hours for Lovesta to come to live with her.

"I will not bring disgrace on thy house," Lovesta asserted in that new hard voice she had.

"Thee cannot bring disgrace when thee has no fault," Lydia answered.

"Thee would lose thy friends."

"If my friends fall away from thee, they are no true friends," said Lydia the valiant.

At last, almost by physical dragging, she came to Lydia's house.

Wonderful how the presence of the young folk healed her. Jane was in love with Gideon Whippy across the street, and Lovesta never tired of watching the progress of the courtship. Little lame Rosie came to her for comfort and Dionis came to her for stories.

Dionis, big girl though she was now, seemed never to sense that Aunt Lovesta was defeated. When the family were gathered about the fire and other young folk came in, Dionis was sure to ask her to tell of that time she saved the young girl from a foreign ship, that time she stopped the burly giant from beating his son in the New York street and then found a new home for the little boy.

Lovesta would begin timidly but would soon be in midstream of the story with the children all listening openmouthed.

Wherever Aunt Lovesta came, came always adventure. Sometimes the adventure was of her own making, sometimes it seemed attracted by her mere presence, as the magnet draws the needle.

After Aunt Lovesta had been at the house some months and her face had grown a little brighter, the adventure began.

Jetsam awoke with a start in the middle of the night, thinking Injun Jill was prowling about with her candle. He jumped up and ran into the kitchen. There was prowling, certainly, but the prowlers were Aunt Lovesta and Mrs. Coffyn, and each held a sputtering candle. About them the shadows retreated into the abysses of the great kitchen.

"Is thee quite sure?" asked Lydia excitedly.

"Oh, yes! I never had a surer leading. I was broad awake when it came. It seemed as though I had been wakened to receive it. And instantly there was borne in upon my mind, 'Someone is hungry.'"

"'Someone is hungry,'" repeated Lydia. "But who can it be?"

"I do not know that," said Lovesta. "But someone is hungry. That I know, and deeply distressed, too."

"Then we must make haste," said Lydia commonplacely.

Jetsam found voice at last.

"Be somebody sick?" he questioned. "I kin go an' git Dr. Brown."

"No, child," said Lydia, opening the bread box. "We must provide food, that is all."

"Not merely food, but a good meal," insisted Aunt Lovesta. "I'll call Stephen to kill a chicken."

"If thee ever can wake him," said Lydia. "He may object, too."

Jetsam looked from one to the other. He didn't in the least know what it was all about, but he determined to be part of it.

"I kin git a chicken easy," he said. "I used to steal 'em fur Injun Jill."

"I hope thee doesn't steal them any more!" said Lydia.

"Why, no," was his innocent answer. "I got a plenty now."

"Well, hurry," said Lydia. "Get thy clothes on quick. Shoes and socks, remember. It's cold yet. Try to get an old hen."

In a few short moments, Jetsam was making his way to the chicken house. The yard looked unreal, like a place never seen before. As he came out, the South Tower clock struck one doomful stroke into the misty silence. It was shivery. Jetsam must have lost some of his skill as Jill's pupil, for the chicken squawked dreadfully when he caught it. What a fool thing to be killing a chicken at one o'clock at night. He hastily got himself back into the house.

Dionis was in the kitchen, wrapped in a cloak.

"What is it?" she asked. "Mother, why is thee getting breakfast in the night time?"

"It isn't breakfast, child," said Aunt Lovesta. "I have a concern to feed someone who is hungry."

"Who?"

"I don't know. I must go out and find them."

"Oh, Aunt Lovesta, let me go, too, on thy errand for God. Thee always said thee'd let me go sometime."

"No, Dionis," Lydia began, afraid that Lovesta would be hurt at this reference to the forbidden journeys.

"Let her go, Lydia. Who knows what she may learn? I shall feed the hungry even if I cannot preach. Jetsam, can thee hitch the horse?"

"Yes, ma'am." Jetsam's eyes were round with amazement. "I kin drive 'er, too."

Presently the kitchen smelled like midday—the chicken roasting on the spit, the fire crackling under the pot, the coffee boiling.

"Huh!" muttered Jetsam. "Somebody's hungry now, fer sure. An' not hard to find, nuther."

Presently all the good things were packed in a basket, and presently again Jetsam was driving old Betty clattering down the deserted street.

An upper window was thrown open and Mr. Joy's nightcapped head popped out.

"What's all the noise?" he shouted. "Is there a fire? Wait, I'll get my bucket."

"No," called Aunt Lovesta's rich voice. "I have a concern, that's all."

The window banged down again; but not before the neighbor was heard to mutter, "Thee and thy concerns! Don't see why thee couldn't have 'em by day."

"Where to?" Jetsam questioned.

"I feel for the Polpis road," said Aunt Lovesta dreamily.

Jetsam allowed himself a low whistle and slapped the reins.

As soon as they cleared the town, they entered a veritable fairyland. A dry mist, more usual in the fall than now in spring, lay low upon the land. Everything was veiled in pearly fog, but the sky was clear, the moon shining, and even the stars. The fog was curiously radiant. The road skirted the swamps east of the harbor—the intense smell of the sea. They saw the riding lights of vessels and Brant Point Light sprayed into foggy aureoles of lustre; on the other side of the road the moors stretched into infinity. Sometimes the mist in the hollows shined upon by the moon was like white lakes.

The cart rattling along was the only sound. Dionis was in the ecstasy of adventure. It was as good as going to the Cape.

She and Aunt Lovesta sat on chairs in the cart, and Jetsam stood to drive. They came to the Monomoy road and Jetsam mischievously turned into it. Instantly Aunt Lovesta's hand was on his arm.

"I said the Polpis road," she corrected him.

"Gosh," he muttered. "Awful sure, ain't she!"

Now, suddenly, Jetsam saw a ghostly nodding shape in the air above them.

"Oh, Lordy,"—he spoke aloud this time. Then he saw it was the shadow of old Betty thrown into the air by the hanging lantern, and reflected by the mist. All the way this shape hovered over them—unearthly.

"Fool business," Jetsam grunted as he watched it. "How fur we goin' anyways?"

Aunt Lovesta touched his arm again. "There's a light over there," she said. "I think maybe we should have turned up that little road we passed."

Jetsam turned accordingly, took the little road, which soon disappeared, leaving them bumping and lurching over rough turf always toward the light. "Mis' Coffyn" didn't know whose light that was. She was foolish to drive right up to it this way. It might be a lot of sailors with a barrel of rum—or even pirates.

Now they heard the thunder of the surf, dull and deep-toned as it is on Nantucket sands; then gradually another sound mingled with it.

"Listen," said Aunt Lovesta. "Hurry—drive faster."

Sobbing, wild, heartbreaking sobbing, louder and louder with the high frightened crying of children. A hut loomed abruptly in the fog, and before Jetsam could draw rein, Lovesta Coffyn was out and running toward it. Dionis, in perfect trust, and Jetsam, much frightened, followed her.

They pushed open the door. The house light blew out and there was only blackness and the horrible uncontrolled sobbing. Then Jetsam's lantern showed a woman on a low bed, her arms surrounding three children like a hovering mother hen. She screamed as the lantern flashed in.

Lovesta went to her and laid her hand on the cowering shoulder.

"What ails thee? I've come to help," she said.

A surge of some jargon broken with sobs was the only answer, but Jetsam understood the Portuguese of Nan-tucket docks.

"Lord A'mighty," he faltered. "She's sayin' she's starved. No vittles for three whole days an' only a little water. Oh, Lordy, an' ye kept sayin' someone was hungry."

He stood there with his mouth open. But Dionis dashed out for the basket. In a moment it was opened and the children gnawing at the food like dogs. Jetsam fought back a sudden wave of tears. He'd eaten that way so many times. The mother started to eat and then fainted. Then Jetsam had to run down to the beach for water, which Aunt Lovesta dashed into the poor creature's face. When she came to, she showed them her broken leg, told how she had broken it going to the spring in the hollow. "I couldn't get out for food," she told them, with Jetsam for interpreter. "My man, he brought us here a week ago. Then he ran away 'cause there was so many children."

"Why did he run away from children?" queried the astonished Dionis.

"Because he was a brute, I'm afraid," said Aunt Lovesta. "But hurry, child. Thee can help."

Then what excitement—what deep, absorbing, exciting pleasure—putting all to order and making the woman and the poor little brown babies comfortable. Aunt Lovesta worked and made everybody else work, too. Jetsam ran down to the misty beach for driftwood.

Dencey swept the room and Jetsam lighted the fire. Oh, happy activity! And all the while Jetsam's reason was standing amazed and trying to deny all of it.

"Hit just happened," he said doggedly. "Mis' Coffyn couldn't wake up in her bed and know they wus hungry way out here."

"How did you know to come?" the woman asked.

"The Lord told me," said Aunt Lovesta simply.

"But I didn't say any prayers," said the woman.

"Sometimes the Lord hears prayer before it is uttered," said Aunt Lovesta.

It was hours before they left the hut to drive home in the fog that was paling into the early dawn of spring.

What news they had to tell the waiting Lydia and the astonished family when they all came down to breakfast.

40. *A Royal School*

WITH THE COMING of Jetsam into the bosom of the family, Dionis, curiously enough, lost him. He didn't even look as he used to. He shot up tall as the months went by. They could see him grow. And he developed a boyish grin that showed all his white teeth, exasperatingly merry. No, Dionis never regained that starved needy person who waited for her in the Commons. Jetsam joined the ranks of the boys in the house— Bob, Kanah, and Steve—who teased Dionis.

Only Jetsam's teasing was different—more trying and continuous.

"Aw, let me carry yer books," he would insist as she started to school.

"Why should I? I'm no baby, I won't drop them."

"Aw, go long, let me. They're heavy for ye."

"They're not, either."

He followed her out to the street, and, in a moment when she wasn't looking, he snatched the books and marched along beside her, grinning that don't-care grin of his.

"Thee give them to me, Sam Jetsam. What'll folks think?—thee walking with me this way."

"That's just it. I want them to think it."

Dionis blushed wrathfully. "But thee isn't, Sam Jetsam."

"I'm not what? I never said I was anything." And his eyes would seem to light upon her like winged things come to rest. Then he looked away.

"I am yer beau, too. Ye hain't got no other one."

"I don't want any beau, I tell thee. And I wouldn't have a—a fairy prince on a silk cushion if he said, 'hain't got no.'"

It was Jetsam's turn to get red.

"Damn—I mean darn it. I wish I talked right. I try an' try. I'm as common as pig tracks, I guess."

Then, worse luck, Dionis was sorry for him.

"Thee isn't common, and I don't think so."

"Ye don't! Say, I'm darn glad ye don't. I'd—I'd ruther ye'd think it than anybody, honest!"

Again that look of his blue eyes which Dencey "wished he wouldn't." It made her so uncomfortable.

Again and again was this fight about his going to school with her. That is, to the school door, for of course Jetsam could not go to the Coffin school. He was not of the blood royal.

Now that he was well and strong, Lydia took cognizance of this.

She went industriously to get him a place at the Fragment School. Poor Lydia.

"He is quite gentled now," she told them, "and an extremely bright lad. He insists on learning Dionis's lessons with her every evening. I don't see how he keeps up with the class, for he has had no instruction. And he reads every book he can find in the house, no matter what it is. He reads them too quick, but the school here can correct that."

At last they consented to take him, and Lydia returned triumphant. She called Jetsam into the keeping room.

"Thee is to go to the school to-morrow," she told him. "They are willing to take thee now."

Jetsam's face flushed out a joyous pride.

"Will they take me in Dencey's class? I know I could keep up."

"Oh—thee isn't going to the Coffin School. Thee can't go there. It's the Fragment School."

Jetsam's face changed to the blackest anger Lydia had ever dealt with.

"I won't go thar," he said loudly.

"But thee must. Thee must be grateful for such school-ing."

"I won't go, I tell ye," his voice was fierce from keeping back the tears.

"Look here, Samuel. No boy or girl ever answers me that way. Thee shall not say 'won't' to me."

Jetsam swallowed hard. He looked at her desperately.

"All right, I won't say it, Mis' Coffyn. But——"

"Thee will go, then, to-morrow?"

He shut his lips tight and shook his head.

"Why not?"

"I don't belong with them thar."

"Any boy who says 'them thar' certainly does belong with them. Pride is a very foolish thing."

His eyes stung. His anger spoke wildly.

"Then I'll go away from hyar. I'll live with Dicky Dicks. He won't make me larn with the low-downs."

Lydia was astonished at this outbreak. Astonished at her own weakening before it. Could she let him go away—this boy who had saved Dencey's life?

Like an instinctive dog, he felt the break in her will. He began to plead.

"Ef ye'll let me go to the Coffin School, I'll scrub the floors. I don't mind. An' I don't never need to answer in class like them. I'll jest set still in the back, and Dencey'll let me say lessons to her evenin's. I—I won't belong ef they don't want me. Couldn't I scrub the floor 'stead o' old Noose? He's an Indian."

In utter puzzlement, Lydia laid the matter before Tom. "The boy was really dreadful. He's never acted like that before. I—I thought he cared to live here."

Tom laughed and kissed her.

"There—there," he said. "Thee's not expected to understand boys, especially a young ruffian like that."

"But, Tom, he swore right before me. It's not a laughing matter."

"I'll deal with him," said Tom.

But the Captain soon got at the heart of the matter.

"Bless his pride," he said, coming back from the long talk with Jetsam. "The boy's got grit. That's all. He won't learn from charity and he won't be thrown with the low class of boys. I'm astonished, Lydia, that thee'd want him to go back and forth from them to our children."

When Aunt Lovesta heard of it, she had a fine plan.

"I'll adopt the boy," she said, "and he can be called Coffyn. Then maybe they'll let him in."

But here was another rock to wreck on.

"I wunt be called Coffyn," Jetsam asserted.

"Why on earth not? Doesn't thee like the name?"

"Yes, oh, yes, hit's the best name they is. But—that's the reason."

"What reason?"

Jetsam blushed painfully.

"I think now, young man, thee is acting foolish," said Aunt Lovesta.

Of course he was acting foolish. He knew it to the bottom of his heart. But how could he tell Mrs. Lovesta that he was going to marry Dencey and so must have a different name from hers?

"What is the Indian woman's name? You might take hers."

"Okorwaw. What kind of a name is that for a white man?" said Jetsam with dignity. (Imagine calling Dencey Mrs. Okorwaw!)

Jetsam's face grew wistful.

"I wisht I had a name, I do so. I don't belong to Indian Jill. She lies when she says it."

And Lovesta, in real pity for the boy, said nothing.

In the end, it was arranged as Jetsam had planned it. He swept and scrubbed the floors at the Coffin School instead of Hed Noose who had long been too old for the job. He listened in class from the back of the room.

Surely no royal university could out-royal the Coffin school. No Off-Islander could possibly know the seal of respectability it set upon its own. Founded by Admiral Sir Isaac Coffin, Bart., as a gift to his kin on the Island, it was to be attended only by true descendants of the original Tristram Coffin. A census had been taken, and five hundred of these privileged children had been found. When certain men of the General Court wished to omit Sir Isaac's titles from the charter, the baronet threatened to recall his gift. Therefore "Admiral Sir Isaac Coffin's Lancastrian School" was its name.

No wonder Injun Jill's Jetsam could not be enrolled among its pupils.

Jetsam always went out before the class was dismissed, and went home alone. He did not belong, but he learned as those who hunger and thirst after learning always do.

41. *Beaux!*

IN ALMOST EVERY Quaker household is to be found one person who hungers for color—just physical bright color which Quakerism denies to its devotees. Dionis was such a person.

As she came to be fourteen and fifteen years old, this longing for color was like starvation. The green of the grass in the spring seemed to rise upward—a shining emanation from the sward. Bright flowers drew her with a pull as of gravity itself. Love is said to be of the nature of identity. And no doubt there was bright color in Dencey's soul.

In all such color love there is the urging to deal with the color—to re-form it into some creation of one's veritable own. Dionis's creativeness prompted her to strange activities.

She took out again the bright colored shells her father had brought from the Pacific, made "flower pieces" of them—the best that any of the schoolgirls made. But she disliked the "pieces" when finished and broke them up.

She even tried to make a little human figure of the

shells, using tiny black periwinkles for eyes and lined bits of scallop shells for fingers. Her imagining of this figure beforehand was a lovely youth. It turned out a decrepit old man and made her furious. Most of the girls at school longed for bright dresses, discussed them secretly. But Dionis had no wish that way. The thing was too intimate for "vain shows."

One day she brought in a huge armful of red flowery branches. She had climbed a tree to get them, an unheard-of performance for a girl of fifteen. She decked her room with them as if for a wedding feast—mantelshelf, window frames, dresser, the head, the foot of the bed. Then she sat down in the midst of it.

So Lydia found her.

"Such extravagance, Dionis. I am ashamed of thee. And thy room covered with twigs. Take it down at once."

And, after much protest, Dionis did so. But when her mother burned them in the kitchen fire, she wept and stormed like a frightened child.

"Thee's turning them all gray, Mother," she shouted. "They're shriveling."

After such an outburst Dionis would be specially cross with Jetsam. To be sure, he was always provoking her, tweaking her hair, pulling at the yarn of her spinning wheel and tangling it, never leaving her alone.

"Thee acts like a baby, Sam Jetsam," she told him. "Why, even Ariel has got more sense than thee."

That summer, with the suddenness of a tide turning, Dionis and Hopestill came to the age of beaux. Hopestill was six months younger. But she "had a beau" first—one beau—Ed Dewsbury. He would walk in the lanes with her and hold her hand. And once he even kissed her.

"I think Ed Dewsbury's the handsomest boy in the whole Coffin School," she told Dionis. "Did thee ever notice his shining locks?"

"Shining bear's grease," said Dencey. "His hair's just plastered with it. It smells up the whole schoolroom."

"It doesn't, either. Anyway, that's violet perfume. Which boy does thee like best?"

"I don't like any of 'em. Not a single one. They haven't one of 'em got any sense. They're just idiots, boys are."

Lydia, coming suddenly into the room, caught the last sentence.

"Dionis, what a thing to say. Thee knows poor Billy Untold. He's an idiot. I am sure none of our boys are like that."

"Well," she conceded. "They don't wiggle their mouths like him. But they *are* idiots, Mother—they never say a single thing that's got any sense."

"Dencey, Dencey!"

"I don't care, Mother. I wouldn't care if I didn't see one of them for years and years and years."

Dionis actually thought this was true. She had no chance to find out whether she'd miss them or not. The boys saw to that. As to their "having sense," Dionis's judgment was not far from the truth.

There were three boys in the running—perhaps even a fourth. Bob Merrill generally managed to walk home from school with her.

He it was who offered her a "sentiment candy."

Dionis opened it, half expectation, half shyness, well knowing what would be inside.

She unwrapped the tiny ribbon of paper from around the gumdrop and read aloud the printed couplet:

"'However fair thou art, remember this,
That grisly death must follow bliss.'"

"But I'm not fair," she objected. "I'm the blackest girl in school."

Bob snatched the candy back. "That's not the one. That's religious." He popped that candy into his own mouth and gave her another. "That one's for thee."

This revealed the time-worn lyric:

"Roses are red and violets blue,
  Sugar's sweet and so are you."

"Bob Merrill, I'm ashamed of thee," Dionis declared. "I like the 'grisly death' one better. At least it's true."

That night she asked her father if "grizzly" always meant a bear, and he gave the confusing reply that it did.

"But why does thee ask?"

"Oh, nothing, only Bob Merrill's a bigger goose than I thought he was."

Bob Merrill, Richard Hold, or Zekiah Dunham always walked home with Dionis elbowing and tussling with each other for the privilege. But no one ever walked toward school with her but Jetsam.

Bob Merrill tried to once, waiting outside the Coffyn gate until Jetsam and Dionis came out. There followed a quarrel, a struggle—nay, a knockdown fight. Lydia rushed out to find Jetsam sitting astride of Bob and pounding him with his fists.

"Samuel—Samuel—get up—get up at once. I am ashamed of thee, I am indeed."

Lydia had to use all her strength to separate them. She took Jetsam into the house.

"What shall I do with thee? I thought thee was a gentleman now. Doesn't thee know it's wicked to fight?"

"It ain't wicked," retorted Jetsam, his chest heaving with excited sobs. "He called me a no-name Kanaka and a half-breed. I'm not a Kanaka. I'm not a no-name."

"If thee'd taken the Coffyn name Lovesta offered, thee wouldn't be," reassured Lydia.

"But I'm not. I've got a name, only I don't know it."

"I hope so indeed," said Lydia in sudden pity. "But thee mustn't fight. No Friend must fight. It's against Jesus."

"I allus fight. I'm not a Friend."

"Isn't thee my friend?" said Lydia with a faint attempt at humor.

But the "no-name" taunt stayed in Jetsam's mind, a wrong to brood over. He denied it in words, but he knew its truth. Coming home from his work in the cooper shop, milking the family cow, whenever he was lonely, the thing crossed him and hurt him. It matured him because it was no imagined sorrow. It meant trouble ahead.

Somehow, he blamed the trouble on Jill, and the thing focused into more hatred of Jill.

As to his courting, Jetsam had a little more sense than the other boys, but not much. It was Jetsam who scratched Dionis's initials on his arm, and when they healed, Spartanly scratched them open again. At last his arm grew really sore, and Dionis told on him.

After that he saved up his money and had his arm properly tattooed.

"Now," he said, proudly showing the inflamed art piece to his lady love. "Even if I'm lost on a South Pacific Island, they'll know who I belong to."

"No, they won't," said Dencey the literal. "The Fijis can't read."

"Maybe they won't be Fijis, maybe they'll be Tahitians."

To these sailor-bred young folk the Pacific islands were individualized. Fathers and uncles had all been there. Jetsam himself would be there in a year, two years, or three. All boys went to sea.

Jetsam drew down his sleeve over the outspread bird and the letters—

Dionis C

"Maybe they won't read me," he said, grinning. "Maybe they'll just eat me."

"Sam Jetsam, you horrid thing. How can thee even say it!"

He was delighted that she shuddered.

42. *The Husking*

WITH THE AUTUMN came the usual corn husking. A great company of young folk, both Quaker and from the North Church, were invited out to Starbuck's Farm.

A wonderful ride it was out from the cosey town into the wide dreaming mystery of the moors. The moon was about to rise over Quidnet, sending up a rosy blush into the sky like real dawn. The carts laden with young folk clattered along the rut-road. In all the hollows of the moors stole the drawn veils of mist which presently the moon touched to an unearthly shining. Sometimes the carts dipped into mists all shivery, sometimes mounted a rise from which they could see the visionary coast merging into the intense silver of the sea.

Amid the noisy shouting, every once in a while Jetsam heard Dencey's laugh. It wasn't loud, but gleeful, infectious as a baby's.

Now they came into the barn. Lanterns hung from the rafters. The floor was piled high with pale yellow corn-in-husks. Now the boys sat down in a row by the husks and at that, all the laugh and chatter of the girl voices ceased into silence.

The husking was to begin.

All of a sudden a loud shout, "Go!" and every youth reached out lightning-quick. There was a tearing sound like a mighty wind—the golden ears flew in one direction and the husks in another. Such dust, such laughing and confusion. It was the joyfullest time in the whole world. The boy who got the red ear of corn was to kiss the prettiest girl; the boy who husked the most corn was to kiss his sweetheart.

Jetsam made a terrible resolve to husk most corn. Of course, if he got the red ear, he'd kiss Dencey anyhow. He didn't care who thought Hopestill was the prettiest. Victory in the husking—that was his goal. Besides, he'd like to beat those Coffyns and Starbucks and Gardners who held themselves so much higher than he.

A wild laugh went up, a deafening shout. Ed Dewsbury had got the red ear and was chasing Hopestill all about the place to kiss her. Of course, he caught her. The boys always did. And Hopestill blushed crimson at his sounding smack.

Then all turned back to the husking.

But Jetsam had not stopped one moment.

Bob Merrill, over there, had an awful pile of corn. Jetsam glanced through the dust. Yes, it was bigger than his. Suppose Bob Merrill kissed her—kissed Dencey. He'd knock him down. If not now, then to-morrow. He couldn't stand it, if anybody else kissed her.

Oh, the agony of haste—hurry—hurry, hurry. His arms ached and his shoulders. His hands stung. Most of them had given up now and were standing looking at Zeke

Dunham, Bob Merrill, and Jetsam. Jetsam had always been swift-handed. He could take a reef even now as quickly as any ripe sailor.

There, Bob Merrill dropped out—stopped in utter exhaustion. Gracious, would Zeke Dunham kiss her? Never—never. It didn't occur to Jetsam now that anybody would choose to kiss any girl save Dencey.

On and on and on—such a dusty mad race!

The girls crowded closer, clapping first for Zeke, then for Jetsam. Only a dozen husks left. Jetsam snatched them in a daze. Then three, two, one. The husking was over. The judges began counting the ears of corn. Bob's pile, and Zeke's, and Jetsam's.

Jetsam stood wiping the perspiration off with his sleeve. He was a sight to be kissing Dencey Coffyn. He was almost sure he had won. He was hilarious, exulting.

"Sammie Jetsam won!" went the cry. "Pick her out, Sam. Who's thy sweetheart?"

(As if there were any doubt about that!)

"Catch her, Sam!"

The barn rocked with shouting and laughter.

Jetsam looked about for Dencey. There she was, over by the barn door. He ran toward her. Of course she'd dart out into the yard. But that would be all the better.

All this flashed through Jetsam's brain in the instant of his run. Then he reached her.

She did not run away. Not at all. She stood there under the bright lantern; and as he caught her hand she looked at him—just looked quick into his eyes.

Pride, fear, pleading, most of all virgin shrinking were in the look. It excluded him like a sudden ghost.

Before Jetsam knew it, he had dropped her hand.

"All right. I won't," he whispered.

And he darted out into the moonlight of the yard.

43. *The Half-Breed*

JETSAM WALKED HOME in a veritable war-fare. Down deep in his heart he knew Dencey was right. He couldn't kiss her like that before everybody, as if it were peeling potatoes. Ed Dewsbury had kissed Hopestill. But Dencey! He wondered if he would ever dare kiss her at any time or at any place.

But equally down deep in his heart Jetsam was angry, furiously angry and furiously hurt. She might have just kissed him, anyway. She knew what people would say. He knew also. How bitterly he knew. "That Jetsam boy of Injun Jill's. Of course Dencey Coffyn wouldn't let him kiss her. The boy himself had sense to see he couldn't—a half-breed Indian with no name."

That's what he was. Dencey believed that, and that was the reason she did not let him. Jetsam knew perfectly well this wasn't so, yet it fed his anger. It fed his pain. She might have saved him the humiliation. She hadn't saved him. And he'd won the kiss in fair rules of the game.

He came into the gate of the Coffyn home as miserable a human being as might be.

He didn't want to meet anybody. It was early yet, and the front windows of the house still lighted. He stole into the back door and through the dark kitchen to his room, where he threw himself fully dressed on the bed.

He had lain there for perhaps a half hour, the slow shamed tears gathering in his eyes, which he exasperatedly rubbed away against the coverlet, when Captain and Mrs. Coffyn came into the kitchen. The candlelight flashed through the crack of his door ajar.

"I must turn over the yeast," said Lydia. "You know it might produce spontaneous combustion."

"I wonder if that's possible," said Tom interestedly. "Spontaneous combustion."

Jetsam could hear Lydia scraping up the cornmeal yeast from the table with a spoon.

"Of course, we must be fair in the matter," said Captain Coffyn, as if opening up some subject again.

"Yes—yes, at least—that," answered Mrs. Coffyn thoughtfully.

"But we must be fair to Dionis, too," said the Captain.

At the word "Dionis," Jetsam pricked up his ears.

"I wouldn't worry about Dencey," Lydia was saying. "She doesn't care the least for boys. Why, she calls them idiots."

"She cares for them, Lydia, or they wouldn't be around her so much. And she cares for the boy Sam most of all. She never thinks of doing her lessons without him. They are together every evening. Suppose she should want to marry him?"

"Well, Tom, he saved her life, remember that."

"Saving her life doesn't give him the right to spoil it

afterward." Captain Coffyn's voice rose with distinct severity.

Jetsam was aware of a sudden thrust that made all the other wrongs as nothing. He lifted his face. There were no tears any more. He hardly noted Lydia's answer.

"But, oh, Tom, if thee had been here when it happened. If it hadn't been for Samuel, we wouldn't have any daughter to marry or give in marriage."

"There isn't a young fellow in Nantucket fit for Dencey, anyway—not one," said the proud father. "And this boy. Of course, he's bright and all that, but—but—why, he may be an Indian half-breed. He's certainly ill-born. Think of the bad inheritance he'd bring into the family—drunkenness, vile temper, and worse. Impossible! Can't thee see?—it's impossible."

"He is a good lad," said Lydia softly.

But Jetsam did not hear her say it. He had wildly stopped his ears and hid his face. His whole mind was in a tumult of hurt—the fresh, poignant suffering of the young, who don't know what to do with that terrific stranger.

They didn't want him here, the Coffyns, here in this beautiful house. How could he ever have imagined they would? They were afraid of him as if he might touch them with disease.

They were especially afraid for Dencey. No wonder Dencey wouldn't kiss him. She, too, was afraid. She was thinking of his hidden disgrace.

He was the son of Injun Jill.

Jetsam was wrecked on unexpected rocks. What should he do, where turn! He mustn't stay here if they didn't want him. Must he go back to Injun Jill?

"No!" he said aloud and beat his fist on the bed. Then he looked, terrified, at the door. But the crack was black. They had gone. Oh, they must never know that he was here and had listened to them. For the first time it dawned on Jetsam that eavesdropping was an ungentlemanly thing.

Now he could not tell them he was going away. Then they'd know he had heard. It would shame Captain Coffyn, it would shame Mrs. Coffyn. She might try to explain. Oh, never, never, never! All his boy-shyness was in revolt against the scene. He couldn't plan. He couldn't think except to repeat Captain Coffyn's sentences, which seemed to burn shame into him. ("A half-breed. Drunkenness and worse.") Oh, he must go away!

He thought of Dicky Dicks's. Should he go there? The rough surroundings—smell of stale liquor, the coarse things he knew were going on. Jetsam turned from Dicky Dicks's with loathing.

And of course the thought of the sea—that first refuge for the Nantucket boy. Jetsam knew sea life as well as though he had lived it. He knew its cruelties and he knew its vast adventure. He was surely going some day, no Nantucket youth dreamed of anything else: but he wanted to go with the right sort of captain. Four years with the wrong captain meant tragedy. The barque *Demeter* was sailing next week with the cruelest captain on the Island. He wouldn't go in her.

He'd get a little room down by the docks. He could pay for it with his wages at the cooper shop. But what would he tell Mrs. Coffyn about his going? If he went away, she'd guess why.

Jetsam found himself at an impasse. A grown man would have flung out of it and let the Coffyns guess what they would. Jetsam was sixteen—at least (no one knew his age) he seemed about that.

Sixteen in boy or girl is delicate and shrinking as a wild-wood creature—intensely and jealously alone.

44. *A Stranger in the House*

JETSAM STAYED. Stayed through a refined torture in the Coffyn home.

He ate his meals in silence and kept away other times. He utterly refused to sit with Dencey in the evening learning lessons. He spent long hours in his room, longer hours out of the house, where, the Coffyns did not know.

Dencey missed him dreadfully. Of course, she was too proud to let him know it. That Jetsam should be so offended about the matter of the kiss seemed to her utterly unfair. He acted as if it were his right to kiss her and she had deprived him of a right. No boy had a right to kiss her and no boy ever should. It was silly.

Sometimes the distress in his eyes touched her.

"I can't get that sum in fractions, Jetsam," she ventured shyly. "Won't thee help me?"

And so he helped her. He sat with her on the bench by the fire, holding the book at arm's length. He explained all the ins and outs of it with care, and wrote the figures.

"You understand it now, don't you?" he asked. And rose without waiting for answer. The formality of the whole performance was almost an insult. As he left the room, Dencey's eyes stung with tears.

Lydia would stop him in the hallway asking him not to go out. Poor Lydia was accustomed to have people return coldness for her kindnesses. She seemed to be made that way. She blamed herself.

Tom thought the boy had got into bad company.

As to Jetsam, all his brooding followed two paths—a hatred of Injun Jill and a gloomy consciousness of sin.

That look of Dencey's there under the lighted lantern had revealed—among so many things it told him—an abyss of purity that he had never dreamed of.

Dencey was stainless, innocent of all the filthy things he knew. Innocent of matters he had touched and handled, not knowing how filthy they were. There at Injun Jill's—the foul oaths she had flung at him—the oaths he had flung back. At Dicky Dicks's the stories he had heard and laughed at, though he had always liked best the tales of breathless escapes and adventures. All these were revealed to him now in horror. No wonder Dencey wouldn't have him. He was black, black, black.

He walked alone in the wind of the Commons, the wind cutting his face as these thoughts cut his heart.

He believed in God. Practically everybody did then. But in the Coffyn household, God had gradually loomed up to Jetsam a very real Person. Kind to them, but distant and awful to himself. He began to fear God and hell.

And all this dire change in his life was due to Injun Jill. Unreasonably he thought that. His hatred of her grew and grew until he could actually taste it in his mouth.

One day, tramping on the Commons, he met her face to face.

He made the first onslaught.

"You, Jill Okorwaw," he shouted. "What ye mean, callin' me yer son? I hain't, I tell ye. I hain't yer son. Ye hear?"

Jill stared, dazed, as if at first she did not know him. Then her sleepy Indian look changed to the Indian glare. She had only those two expressions.

"Yes—ye air my soon," she yelled back. "All mine."

"I hain't neither, an' ye've got to stop sayin' it. I don't belong to ye." Jetsam stamped on the ground. "I never did. Not noways." His old rough speech returned to his tongue. "I was shipwrecked. An' ye know about it an' ye won't tell. Ye've got to tell me, darn ye!"

"I tellth," she nodded her head. "Ye b'long me. Al—ways!" She chuckled. She was three parts drunk and smelt horrible. "First day ye coom, ye crawlth away, quick. Get away fro' Indion Jeel. But I ketch, an' hol' tight—my baby."

It was the first break Injun Jill had ever made. It gave Jetsam a wild ray of hope.

"Thar," he cried. "I told ye. I'm not yourn. A baby couldn't crawl the first day it come. No baby could." He laughed suddenly.

"Ye air mine, too. I hol' ye so." Jill crooked her two arms as if the baby were within them. She held it close against her breast.

To children—and Jetsam had yet the child in him—the mother relationship is intense. No thinking mitigates it. It is all emotion.

That gesture revolted Jetsam—that he should have been like that with Injun Jill.

"I hain't, I hain't," he cried out chokingly. "Ye're a old foul Injun hag. Ye're dirty an' drunk and——"

Jill's clumsy tenderness changed to her Indian glare.

She darted forward and struck Jetsam, aiming at his head but hitting his shoulder. And in a flash he struck her back, a terrible blow on the cheek.

She grunted with pain.

Instantly, as he struck her, he seemed to have an instinctive sense that she was his mother. He had struck his mother!

He turned and ran in mortal fear. Ran out into the lonely sheep pastures.

Yes, he was Jill's son. He showed it. Hadn't he sworn and blasphemed like her, hadn't he struck her—a woman? Yes, he was low and ill-born. Just Jill's. That was all.

He felt a thousand leagues away from the dear Coffyn household and atmosphere. An absolute stranger.

45. *The Friendly Dicky Dicks*

BUT AS HE TRUDGED back to town Jetsam began to think more reasonably.

Jill had made a break—that was sure. If he hadn't been so wild and lost his temper, he might have led her on to say more. To say something that would really assure him that he was not hers.

Oh, how he hated her!

He could ask Dicky Dicks. Perhaps he would remember about it. Injun Jill was so unimportant and lived so far out that nobody noted one way or another about her baby. There was the wreck of the *British Queen* long ago. And there was the rumor, chiefly recounted by Nantucket children for its romantic flavor, that Jetsam had been taken off that wreck. The Fragment boys had dubbed him Jetsam for that reason.

Yes, he would ask Dicky Dicks.

He found his way down to the ill-odored grog shop which he had kept aloof from so many months. Dicky was inclined to be hurt.

"'Shamed of yer old friends, hain't ye?" he queried. "Now the Tom Coffyns have taken ye up."

"I'm not ashamed of you, Dicks," said Jetsam, and realized that it was true. The Coffyns were ashamed of him, but he wasn't of Dicks, who had been good to him.

Dicks could see that the boy was in trouble and soon softened.

They sat down by the fire. The customers were gone. Then, trembling for the reply he might get, Jetsam asked his question.

"No, I don't reckon ye're Jill's kid," answered Dicks. "But ye hain't no better off ef ye hain't. 'Cause then ye're Bill's."

Bill was the man who had lived with Jill in Jetsam's earliest childhood. Then he had gone to sea.

"Bill," repeated Jetsam miserably.

"Yes, I reklect the hull thing. Bill was wrecked on the *British Queen*. Everybody was so busy salvigin' wreckage, they didn't notice about him much. But he come trampin' across the Common in the middle o' the night to Jill's door with ye, a mite of a baby, in his arms. Ye can't tell me that Bill would 'a' saved ye ef ye hadn't ben his'n. Besides, he said ye wus his. When he fust come and folks down hyar tried to git 'im to tell about the wreck, he'd never talk. He allus looked skeered. He said yer ma died at sea 'cause of the storm, and he brung ye with him. Then he'd allus add about ye bein' precious to 'im. Hit never sounded real, that part didn't."

"I should think not," said Jetsam. "I remember his beatings. I was little, but I remember 'em."

"But I don't see why he should claim ye ef ye wasn't his'n. Ye wasn't much to look at."

"But why should Jill claim me, too?" said Jetsam.

He sat staring at the fire. There seemed no way out. He was the hated brat of somebody, any way he made it. Reckon Captain Coffyn was right about his inheriting bad tendencies. And he still hated Injun Jill. Bill had been forgotten. But Jill kept up her claim on him. He thoughtfully felt his nose. Yes, his nose was like Injun Jill's—aquiline like hers.

Just then a crew of sailors came in from a coastwise schooner. They crowded around the bar clamoring for drink and Dicks hurried to wait on them. Jetsam lent Dicks a hand in the work. Why shouldn't he come and stay here with Dicks? Dicks liked him. Perhaps if Jetsam helped him this way, Dicks would keep him for nothing. The men were jolly.

They all sat down on the benches, drinking and talking. Then singing, as the drink mounted to their heads. Jetsam lingered as he used to do in the old time. Didn't he belong here, anyway? The Coffyns didn't want him. Dicks gave him a drink.

If Tom Coffyn had seen him now, his belief as to the bad company would have been verified.

The men grew rougher, quarrelsome. An old sailor started up a chanty, one of the vilest on the coast where many a chanty was vile. Jetsam listened to the verses. He used to know it by heart, he used to laugh at it. But in the midst of one verse, especially coarse, Dencey's pure virgin look stole across his brain like a veil.

He stumbled up from his seat, knocking over his chair. He fairly fled into the street. Into the cold, breathable air. He felt as though he had been wallowing in mud.

46. *The Springtide of the Spirit*

IN THAT WINTER, amid snow and ice, a strange "springtime" dawned over Nantucket. Such "springs" were not uncommon in New England villages. They might come at any season.

They were called "Revivals."

They were not prepared for or invited save in the continual invitation of the earnest spirit which was an integral part of New England life.

There was no invited preacher, no multiplying of church services with impassioned pleas to come to the mourner's bench, no artificial "Revival" such as is known to-day.

The thing just happened. As though on a fertile field a warmth had stolen over, and in response the life, stored and fostered there, sprang up. First a tender green leaf in a corner, then a sudden flower somewhere else, then flowers more and more, until the field was white to the harvest.

Then the whole little community tucked away among New England hills, or islanded in the sea, cut off from the outside world, rocked with news. Important news!

News of the Spirit.

Such a springtime came now over the Quakers of Nantucket. Nobody expected it. Life had been going on rather dully for some months.

Then, suddenly, Martha White was "tendered to the Lord."

All those years since the death of her husband and son, Martha White had been in rebellion. She had been poor and kept a shop in Petticoat Lane, where she served her customers in grim silence, or with a frown and cutting speech. Lately she had been, if possible, more silent and withdrawn.

Then, one morning in First Day meeting, when they had been sitting silent for almost an hour, the vaporing breaths of the worshipers ascending sacrificially in the bitter cold air, Martha rose and spoke.

Her voice was like a sudden bell. A sweet clangor in it never heard before. The whole meeting quivered as if swept by a motion of wind.

"The Lord has called me," rang the sweet unknown voice. "He has called me from rebellion and a bitter battle in myself. He has called me from Hate into His Way of Peace. Blessed, Blessed art Thou, Dear Lord, dear beyond all."

Her voice grew not louder but softer as she thus spoke to her God, as though He were too near for loud speech. It trembled with utter tenderness.

"Thou hast given back my dear ones who were gone. Thou hast given them to my love and my faith. I will wait, Lord. All my life waits upon Thee. O Lord, my help and my shield."

Then she sat down.

The silence trembled for a moment, then Lydia arose and began the Forty-seventh Psalm. Lydia always said the Psalms as though they were her own, given her fresh and warm from God.

"Oh, clap your hands, all ye people." When she came to the phrase, "God is gone up with a shout, the Lord with the sound of a trumpet," one seemed to see the shouting joyousness of God, hastening to the one sinner that had repented.

"Then the watery cloud overshadowing their minds broke into a sweet abounding shower of celestial rain and the greatest part of the meeting was broken together, dissolved and comforted in the same divine and holy Presence."

Such was the Quaker meeting when the Presence of the Lord was upon it.

The folk went home in little excited groups telling the news.

(And we call the New England village dull and colorless.)

The next First Day, who but big Stephen should be touched with the divine fire. Then three young girls who lived on State Street. Then Mary Beck, the seamstress, and Hedassah Gardner and several young men home from a voyage around the Horn. Then people up in the North Congregationalist Church began to get religion.

And then Sammie Jetsam was swept into the spiritual tide.

Of course he had been at the Quaker meetings. No one of the Coffyn household dared absent himself from them. He had heard Martha White with astonishment and fear. He had heard Stephen with envy. And the multiplying of the others with growing faith.

The whole town was full of the excitement. Lovers discussed it in the lanes, women in their kitchens, shipowners in their office, and the cooper at his work. God was not only present, He was fashionable.

Jetsam's mind swung away from his personal wrongs. He began to grope and seek. To Dencey, he was more distant than ever. He noted none of her timid advances, he who once had been so eager to meet them. He walked alone in the Commons, hour long in that spiritual wrestling which has been the experience of all seekers after truth. He tried to find Christ Who, they said, had died for him; he tried to get, if only a touch of the garment hem of that peace which he saw shining in the face of Lydia, and now in Stephen's face, and in the homely, ignorant little face of the seamstress, Mary Beck.

All to no avail. He was outside, a black sheep crying in the darkness. Why was it? Why couldn't he be like those others? What was keeping him back?

It was a misty day, a February thaw, and no snow lying. The fog rolled in broken clouds over the Commons and the whole place seemed asleep.

There, across a dim slope, stood Jill's hut.

When he saw it, Jetsam's whole mind lifted in a veritable shock of hate. Injun Jill pretending to be his mother, making him a half-breed, keeping him from everything that was sweet in life! Then, across the confusion of this, almost like a speaking voice, came the words that Lydia had read aloud that morning.

"He that hateth his brother is a murderer, and ye know that no murderer hath eternal life abiding in him."

His hatred of Injun Jill. That was it. He could never have

God until he gave up that. Why, even now it had shattered all his spiritual longing, filled all his heart with black ink.

"But I can't give that up," he said fiercely under his breath. "I've hated her always, always. Why, I can't remember not hating her. It wouldn't be me."

"All right, then," said his conscience, now suddenly alive and able to speak aloud. "You love your hate of Jill better than you do Jesus, your Saviour. It's a strange choice."

"It isn't a choice. I can't——"

"Thou must."

Hesitatingly he turned around and began to walk draggingly toward Jill's hut. He hadn't any ideas about it, no willingness, no kindness. His face there on the lonely moor was wan and pitiful.

Then, all of a sudden, the thing happened.

The hate died out of him like an old, old pain. It left him free, wholesome—well. A wonderful health he had never known before. He stopped stock still in the path, his mind going deeper and deeper into the Unseen. Curtains were lifted, softly, delicately, deliberately, and beyond each was a greater brightness—a greater joy.

Gradually he knew that something was required of him. He must *do* something. Merely not hating wasn't enough. Quite willingly he started forward again, and, all at once, was at Jill's door.

He pushed it open.

Jill, wrapped in a blanket, sat crouched over a tiny fire. By some singular chance, she was not drunk. He walked over and touched her shoulder.

"Injun Jill, I've—I've come to see you."

She sprang up, fending her head with both arms—a

whine almost like a cat.

A wave of pity engulfed him.

"I won't hurt you, Jill," he said. "I'll never hit you again. Oh, don't be afraid."

But Jill was afraid. Soberness always took all the courage out of Jill, and all her strength. She backed against the wall muttering.

"Ye're foolin'. Ye'll boolst me out my house."

Jetsam was taller than she now by a head. He hadn't noticed it the other day.

"Please don't be afraid," he said again, his voice breaking. And after the pity flowed a stream of love. The poor, miserable, lonely thing! There were almost no Indians left now in the Island. Why, Jill was as alone in the world as he. He saw her in an utterly new aspect.

"You can"—he gulped a little at the difficult word, then went on—"you can be my mother if you want to, Jill. I won't cross you."

She looked up at him with a queer passion in her eyes.

"Ye air my baby," she cried. "Al—ways. B'long no Coffyns. B'long me."

"Yes, Jill," he said quickly. "I belong to ye. I'll get ye some wood. The fire's near out."

He went out to the wood-shed. There, as he picked up the ax, came a scramble and a yelp, and Wash leaped upon him, dragging a rope. Jill had evidently tied him to keep him from running away to Jetsam.

Jetsam untied him while Wash went wild with joy. When Jetsam came in with the wood, the dog was barking, leaping in circles about him.

He built up the fire and filled the poor hut with light and warmth. He opened one window a little to let out the foul air. He seemed to be making the whole place alive.

Jill crouched again by the fire, her face gone into that sleepy stupidity which degenerate Indians had.

It was while Jetsam was sweeping the floor (with the old wreck of a broom) that a new "leading" came to him.

He must stay here with Injun Jill. He must leave the Coffyns and come out here to live with her.

He began to struggle against this. It seemed too much even for the Lord Jesus to ask. But Jetsam did not struggle long. Truly, he was in the hands of the Lord.

He shook Jill gently to rouse her. "I'm goin' to town," he said, "to git you some bread and meat. I'll come again. I'm goin' to stay with you now."

He thought he saw happiness in the leathery old face for a moment.

As he walked toward town, he noticed with wonder that every dry bush, every stalk of old aster or laurel, had rainbow lights about it. He rubbed his eyes and looked again. But the rainbows remained and kept with him all the way.

47. *Jetsam Finds the Clue*

NEXT MORNING, LYDIA, hurrying upstairs to some household duty, found herself stopped at the newel post by Jetsam.

"Samuel, where was thee all last night?" she asked anxiously. "Thee mustn't stay out like that. Captain Coffyn was quite angry."

"I was with Injun Jill," he faltered. "Mis' Coffyn, I'm going to stay with her."

"With Injun Jill? Why, surely—but thee can't be offended. What have we done? Thee mustn't go there, Samuel."

"Yes," he answered, "I must. The Lord, He told me to. Oh, Mis' Coffyn," he broke out suddenly. "The Lord came to me yesterday. He filled me with light—all of me with light."

His eyes became intensely blue, then swam with tears.

"Oh, Mis' Coffyn, I didn't know how good He was!" he said childishly.

Lydia was silent for an instant in sheer surprise of joy. She clapped her hands soundlessly.

"Samuel, Samuel, my dear, dear lad. Oh, I am so happy for thee. Oh, the Lord be praised."

If one of her own had come into the fold, Lydia could not have shown more gladness. She laid her hands over his upon the newel post, looking into his eyes. Jetsam had a rare glimpse of what a real mother might be.

Tom came through the hall.

"Tom, Tom," she called excitedly. "Samuel is saved. The Lord came to him yesterday."

Jetsam, as he faced the Captain, was fairly blinking with embarrassment. But there was no mistaking the blessing in the boyish eyes. Tom's anger and suspicion faded.

"That's splendid, my boy," he said, shaking hands with him. "Thee'll never be sorry for this step."

"It wasn't my step, sir," said Jetsam. "The Lord did the stepping."

Tom laughed but Lydia was a little shocked.

They brought him into the keeping room. They were all there at the morning redding-up. How they gathered around him! Peggy threw her arms about him and didn't seem to mind when he wriggled away. Little Ariel clung to his hand, though he didn't the least know what had happened. Jane said her demure congratulations.

Dionis came running downstairs with the dust cloth. She was the shyest of all.

"I'm glad, Jetsam," she said, and then stood over by the settle watching him, mystified and wistful.

Stephen put both hands on his shoulders in brotherly fashion.

"Thee'll be a Friend now," he said.

"Of course he will," announced Lydia. "Tom, thee'll vouch for him in meeting, won't thee, and I'll talk with

Eliakim and Jonathan Folger. They're on the committee. I'm sure they'll accept thee, Samuel. But thee must answer all their questions straight and true, no matter what they ask."

It was as gay as a wedding.

As he looked about at the beaming faces, Jetsam suddenly realized a new oneness with them. He had tried to enter that circle without the love of God. He could not, for the whole fabric of the family life was founded on that, and without it was no contact.

Now he had the clue.

At first there was a great clamor against Jetsam's going out to live with Injun Jill. Peggy called it a "cryin' shame for a Christian boy to be livin' with that heathen." Jane was shocked. Captain Coffyn told him that he was sure it was unnecessary.

"Thee'll find it hard, my son," he said, "after living here so long."

"It don't seem right for me to say no to you, Captain," answered Jetsam. "But I've got to go."

But he was greatly pleased to be asked. Had even the Captain changed his mind about him?

Only Lydia approved of the going. "It's the price of his peace," said Lydia. "Little enough to do for so great a reward."

All at last grew resigned to it except Dionis.

"It isn't a fit place for thee, Jetsam. Thee knows it isn't. I don't believe she's thy mother. Why, she might kill thee in the night some time when she's drunk."

"She couldn't kill me," he answerd, warming his hope at her solicitude. "Why, I'm twice as strong as she is."

"It's horrid out there. I don't want thee to go."

Oh, delightful this! Jetsam wished that Jill would indeed hurt him. What might not Dencey do then? Why, she might—His whole mind thrilled suddenly at the possibility. He reached out his hand, touching hers on the book, but she immediately drew it away.

It was Dencey who told Lydia about the dirty thin blanket he had and no bed out in Jill's hut. "He told me about it long ago," she said, and insisted on giving him all those from the bed in Jetsam's room. "They're his, anyway," she declared.

Ah, more than the blankets warmed him as he bore them away.

Lydia, seeing Dencey look out from the window as Jetsam disappeared in the darkness, quoted softly:

" 'All things work together for good in them that love God.' " Lydia had the Quaker willingness to follow adventure to the very end.

Not so Tom Coffyn. He viewed these developments in another light.

"This Injun Jill martyrdom has got to stop," he told his wife. "And I'm going to see that it does. The boy shall go to sea."

"Thee'll see that he sails with a good master?" asked Lydia anxiously.

"Yes, I'll manage that. But he must go."

48. *The Chinese Bird Cage*

L IKE MANY martyrdoms, the living with Injun Jill was not so hard in actuality as it had been in contemplation.

Jetsam still went to the Coffin School, doing chores and learning. He still worked at the cooper shop. Happiest of all, he resumed his evening study with Dencey. Then, too, he was now a member of the Meeting. That gave him rights and dignities in the town. He had given his "testimony," frightened at first, then suddenly glowing with the memory of his experience, so that he spoke well. The elders praised him.

After all this, it was not so hard to trudge out over the snowy dark Commons to Jill's cottage. He kept the hut clean, and his earnings gave them sufficient food. Only gradually did Jill seem to believe the change in her life. She began to work hard at her loom.

"No use Coffyn planket," she grunted. "Jeel make planket. My poy, my planket."

"All right, Jill," he said indulgently. "Only I'll have to use the Coffyn blankets until thee gets it done. Thee doesn't want me to freeze."

She was like a child now, and he the adult of the house.

Yes, all that was easy. But the thinking of Jill as his mother—that he found as bitter as ever. It cut him off from Dencey. That wrong was always fresh.

"A half-breed, a half-breed," he would repeat monotonously, as he flung along the lonely path to the cottage. "I can't be that, and I won't be!"

He tried to comfort himself with the cruel Bill. He at least was white. But he and Dicky Dicks's memory of him were vague. Jill was present. After all, Jill had been drunk when she said that about his being a crawling baby. It didn't solve his problem.

Jetsam bought a mirror at a sailor-shop and hung it in Jill's house. It was a source of unending amusement to Jill, who would stand in front of it making faces at herself. Jetsam, too, made faces into the mirror. But they were long faces. He studied his face, feature by feature.

Lordy(Oh, he mustn't say that now that he was a Quaker)—but, Lordy, he was homely. Those high cheek bones! Indians always had 'em—and the nose. It was all right to call it aquiline, but it was like Injun Jill's. And he was always so white. He thought of Dencey's brunette cheeks, not rosy on the surface, but glowing from within. Her eyes so limpid clear which always laughed first before her mouth did. Oh, he wasn't fit to tie her shoe-strings. But he wished he could tie them. He did so! When he was away from her, he always knew he wasn't fit even to talk to her. When he was with her, he was constantly edging and hedging toward love-making.

One day he came into the house with a present for Dencey, the first he had ever given her. He had bought it from a young sailor who had carried it all the way from Canton. Jetsam was trembling a little as he brought it in. It was a bird cage intricately carved of teakwood. Chinese floweres, delicate willow trees, two lovers walking in a garden—all were there in the lace-like structure. And inside it were six beautiful little living birds.

Such unbelievable things wandered into Nantucket harbor.

"Dencey," he called excitedly. "Dencey."

She came running into the keeping room.

"Please take it," he pleaded, holding it toward her. "Please do."

Her eyes lighted upon the lovely thing, and her whole face bloomed with delight.

"Oh!" she said. "Oh——" Then her two arms went around it in an embrace. The tiny birds fluttered in terror, and she withdrew her arms but her eyes still loved it.

"It's the most beautiful thing in the whole world," she said. "How did thee know to find it for me?"

"I always know what thee likes," said Jetsam, soberly watching her.

"Oh, look at the red one," she cried, gazing at the birds. "And the blue one, and the one with the gold-tipped wings. Oh, Jetsam, how pretty!"

This love poured so lavishly upon the birds made him jealous.

"I wish thee wouldn't call me Jetsam," he said crossly.

"Why?" she asked.

"'Cause it isn't a name. A dog could be called Jetsam."

Dencey drew her fascinated eyes from the cage in her first recognition of him.

"That's so," she said. "It's not a nice name and I won't

call thee it again. Not even when I think of thee."

"Oh—does thee think of me?"

"Of course I do, Sam Jetsam. (Oh, there I said it!) I think of Ariel and Mother and Father, everybody——"

"That's not what I mean, Dencey."

"It's what I mean," she maintained.

"I wish I had a name. I do so." He spoke with abrupt unhappiness. "Like Bob Merrill or Blake Folger. I haven't got any—either first name or last."

She was instantly solicitous.

"Thee's got to have a name. Sam is a good Christian name. And what was Bill's name? That man that brought thee from the wreck?"

"I don't know. He was just Bill. He was a cruel man. I remember yet how he beat me till I couldn't stand up. I had to crawl away after it."

Dencey's eyes filled. These pictures of Sam's childhood were intense as anything she knew. And they hurt her.

"I'll tell thee," she said. "Bill found thee in the water, didn't he? Even if thee was his son he had to find thee there. Thee could be Samuel Seaman. I'll call thee that, and I'll make everybody else call thee that, too."

Jetsam studied it, his lips moving in a visible whisper.

"Dionis Seaman. Dencey Seaman." Yes, it was a good name.

"Sam Jetsam, how dares thee!" she cried, stepping away from him as startled as the birds had been.

Yes, she was always like that. She would champion him and plan for him. But she wouldn't let him touch her, not even a little finger.

49. *Off to Sea*

T HEN, SUDDENLY, like the purposeful filling
of a sail, came the greatest event of Jetsam's life.

He was going to sea.

It was providential, so Tom Coffyn thought. Perhaps
he himself was part of the Providence.

One evening, Caleb Severance (Lydia's brother) came
in to talk with Tom. Caleb was sailing next week as captain of the *Sextant*, and had been busy all day with load-
ing the lighters for his ship. The family were about the
fire, and the two captains sat in the circle discussing their
business, when Caleb said:

"Well, some sea-struck youth's going to have a chance
to go to sea. Mary Swain, at the last moment, has bribed
her boy not to go. He was too young anyway—only fourteen. Hasn't thee got some youngster here that would like
to be my cabin boy?"

Elkanah was down-town on an errand, or he would
inevitably have spoken. Jetsam, who was sitting by Dencey
on the settle, looked up at the summons. He hesitated. It
was no small thing to interrupt two captains in their talk.

But at that instant Tom also looked up. Their glances met.

"Would thee like to go, young man?" spoke Tom.

"Oh, Captain, it's the chance I've been hoping for," said Jetsam.

Then what excited busy-ness in the Coffyn household. Lydia asserted that he should buy nothing from the sailor's slop chest. He should have all from her hands as any son would in starting from home. There were the warm flannel underthings to be made, blankets to select from her press, and the few home remedies for cholera and such troubles. Dencey knitted like mad on mittens for him, and Martha White, who had learned tailoring, made the sailor suits.

Jetsam was made a man overnight by his sense of getting started at last. Samuel Seaman, cabin boy, did not look like much on the ship's log. But every youth, poor or rich, had to start at the bottom. The business of whaling was to be learned. And the whale was no respecter of persons. But Jetsam did not intend to return in that lowly position. He was sure he'd be promoted, and to Jetsam it was like becoming a new person.

Dionis was full of joy for him. The *Sextant* was going round the Horn to the Southern Pacific and thence probably to the Japan whaling grounds.

"Only think," she said, her eyes dancing with interest. "Maybe thee'll see Juan Fernandez, where Robinson Crusoe lived, and Easter Island."

"Oh—Easter Island," repeated Sam.

Both young folk knew men who had been there—that most remote morsel of land in the whole world. A thousand miles of sea stretched in every direction about it, yet a series of colossal statues circled its barren shore—all with their backs to the sea. The poor little tribe of Polynesians (a mystery, too, how they got there) knew nothing of the statues, whence they came.

Mystery, adventure, the beauty and wonder of the world were open to Jetsam now.

"Oh, I hope thee'll see Easter Island," said Dionis for the sixth time.

"What I want to see is whales," he answered with a manly swagger.

Then the day came. A sense of fatality about it. Jetsam there among them. Uncle Caleb in his home near by, familiar at the three meals a day. And suddenly they were to be transported into another world—yes, it seemed another planet. They would be invisible for three, four, maybe five years. Perhaps the families would have letters from them, perhaps not. Perhaps their ship would never be sighted. Perhaps——!

But nobody dared to think of that "perhaps" except Lydia, and she in her solitary prayers.

Dionis, as she went about her work dusting and straightening Grandfather's room, had a smothering feeling in her chest. She didn't feel like crying, she was glad of that. But when dinner-time came, she hated the food. She got up busily from the table as if to fetch something from the kitchen, but she went out the back door without shawl or bonnet and walked away to the Commons. She wasn't thinking of Easter Island, or palm trees, or even of the long years of the voyage. She was not exactly thinking of Jetsam. She was only stupid and lonely enough to die.

It was a spring day, a blowing air fragrant with growing things. But the air did not refresh her. The old, old sorrow of Nantucket women had come to her.

She had been walking a long time when there was a strong running step on the turf behind her and Jetsam came up breathless.

"Dencey, why, I've been looking for thee an hour," he said crossly. "Thee wouldn't have let me go without even saying good-bye, would thee?"

"Good-bye?" she questioned.

"Yes. I've barely got time to get to the ship."

She was startled as at the switching sound of a lightning flash. He already wore his sailor clothes. They made him seem like a stranger—real manhood, all of a sudden.

"Is thee angry?" he asked. "I didn't mean to be cross. I—I was afraid I wouldn't find thee."

She looked down and her lips quivered into speech.

"I don't want thee to go."

"Why, I've got to go," he answered. But something in the dogged coldness of her voice sent courage into him.

"Dencey," he said softly. Then all at once he was speaking. "I love thee. I've got to tell thee. I can't help it. I love thee every minute of every day. Oh, even when I'm asleep, I'm loving thee. I couldn't even breathe without thee. Dencey, won't thee love me a little? Oh, won't thee wait till I am come back?"

She looked up. She suddenly knew that this tall, strong, beautiful Jetsam needed her more than had the little boy out in Jill's cottage—more than that ragged, hungry little boy.

Their eyes met. Oh, not as they had met before at the husking. He saw the gentling in her eyes, he saw their thought hovering out toward him, visioning him, and in an instant he threw both arms about her and was kissing her. The bliss was fresh, untried, unknown. He had been protected from it by hate as surely as had she by house-hold love. The invisible world swept them into its realities.

Only a moment. Dionis broke away sobbing. She ran down the path toward home. She did not once look around. She had not said "yes," she had not even said "good-bye." Yet, as she ran, there came upon her again that sense of belonging to Jetsam—the terrible, intimate responsibility for him. She could not tell whether it was intense gladness or intense sorrow.

About the Author

The author, great-granddaughter of Utopian Socialist Robert Owen, was born Cara Dale Parke in New Harmony, Indiana in 1871. The Parkes were a musical family, frequently giving impromptu performances for family and friends, and young Cara assumed that she would become a full-fledged musician. It was after her marriage in 1903 to Charles H. Snedeker, dean of the Cathedral in Cincinnati, that she began the serious study leading to the writing of her first book. A biographical note in *The Horn Book Magazine* by her sister, Nina Parke Stilwell, relates:

"She was happiest while writing, for her characters were companions whom she missed when she finished her books. Before actually writing a story, she would steep herself in the background of her characters; then, as she wrote, they acted of themselves. The author could not force them to act contrary to their way of life. She studied Greek art, literature, religion, and philosophy for six years in preparation for her first book, *The Spartan* [1912], which was laid in ancient Greece. She was a student all her life, even during the latter part when she was bedridden; at 82 she published *A Triumph for Flavius* [1955]."

Raised in a family steeped in progressive ideas of education, the author says that as a child she only received encouragement and admiration; it was her husband who "criticized me wisely and sharply, often making me work months on a single chapter. He also directed my historical studies so I became accurate and sure." *(The Junior Book of Authors)*

Ruth Hill Viguers, in *A Critical History of Children's Literature*, shows how, even in his death, Mr. Snedeker's positive influence was felt. She writes, "It is hard to believe that *Downright Dencey*, with all its vitality, was written in great sorrow. Mrs. Snedeker's husband, who had been her inspiration for her writing, the critic who insisted only on her best, had died, but his faith in her was justified. She created in Dencey the most zestful of all her vivid characters and told a story full of atmosphere and humanity that has been a source of continued pleasure throughout the years."

She has written warmly about her first visit to Nantucket Island—in her later years she lived there part of each year—when she first caught a sense of a book waiting to be written. "I went to Nantucket for a summer visit. As I walked up Fair Street I had a strange feeling: 'There is a story in Fair Street.' It was not at all definite. I did not know that it would be Dencey and Jetsam, and the old whaling captains and the Quakers, but I could feel it there as one senses a perfume one can not see." She goes on to relate about her writing: "I am often asked how I came to write for children. I reply that I do not. I write for myself. I write the story in the best words I know to express the story. If it is simple the words are simple; if it is a complicated subject—and I do write these—I use complicated accurate words. I am never afraid children and young people will not understand me." *(The Junior Book of Authors)*

Though Mrs. Snedeker wrote a number of books that dealt with American history, including three in which figured the New Harmony utopian experiment, her love and preference for the ancient world is clear. Between her first three books about Ancient Greece (*The Spartan, The Perilous Seat* [1923], *Theras and His Town* [1924]) and her last two (*A Triumph for Flavius, Lysis Goes to the Play* [1962]), the author wrote one about a Greek slave in Rome (*The Forgotten Daughter* [1933]), a book about St. Luke (*Luke's Quest* [1947]) and another about early Christianity in Britain (*The White Isle* [1940]).

Caroline Dale Snedeker died in 1957, leaving a legacy of literature still as fresh and accessible for young people of the twenty-first century as it was for those of the century past.

***

Illustrator Maginel Wright Barney, whose chapter heading drawings capture so well the flavor of Nantucket Island in its whaling days, was the mother of Elizabeth Enright, noted author of *Thimble Summer* and many other fine books.